ABOUT ONCE UPON A WINTER

This Christmas, a young woman is about to find out wishes can come true — but in the most unexpected ways.

Weary of city life, Laura Everly moves to the small coastal town of Mistletoe, Maine. A chance visit to a charming antiques shop leads her to an unassuming snow globe she can't resist buying. Unbeknownst to its owner, the snow globe can grant wishes, but they rarely unfold as expected, sending Laura into a maelstrom of joy and confusion.

Farley Cooper is a rugged individualist with an outdoorsy charm that's as intriguing as it is intimidating. He lives by his own rules, and his charismatic aura draws people in one minute while his directness repels them the next.

While Laura's dreams of a perfect Christmas in her new home seem to vanish, deeper feelings for Cooper take their place. But as curious coincidences pile up, doubts arise. Is the snow globe behind them all, including their growing attraction?

Experience the enchantment of *Once Upon a Winter*, a heartwarming reminder of the true magic of Christmas.

GET THE AUDIOBOOK

jljarvis.com/once

Find out more. Scan the QR code.

Highland Passage

Highland Passage
Knight Errant
Lost Bride

Highland Soldiers

The Enemy
The Betrayal
The Return
The Wanderer

Highland Vow

American Hearts

Secret Hearts
Runaway Hearts
Forbidden Hearts

For the latest information, visit jljarvis.com.

Get monthly book news at news.jljarvis.com.

ONCE UPON A WINTER

ONCE UPON A WINTER

A SMALL-TOWN CHRISTMAS ROMANCE

J.L. JARVIS

ONCE UPON A WINTER
A Small-Town Christmas Romance

Published by Bookbinder Press
bookbinderpress.com

ISBN (ebook) 978-1-942767-61-9
ISBN (paperback) 978-1-942767-62-6
ISBN (audiobook) 978-1-942767-63-3

ONE

Laura Everly sighed contentedly as she strolled through the quaint seaside village of Mistletoe, Maine. Crisp, salty air filled her lungs as she wound her way down the main street lined with shops trimmed in twinkling lights. She popped into a bakery and inhaled the spicy aroma of gingerbread. It was exactly the storybook Christmas town she'd dreamed of for her new start.

Up ahead, a display in a shop window caught Laura's eye. It was an antiques store decked out in full holiday splendor. Shimmering snowflakes dangled from the eaves as the warm glow of holiday lights beckoned from within. She had to go inside.

A bell jingled as Laura entered the shop. Immediately, her gaze fell upon a beautiful snow globe on a shelf. Enchanted by the snow-covered village nestled inside the glass globe, she drew nearer. It looked remarkably like Mistletoe. Without hesitation, Laura picked up the snow globe and ran her fingers over the polished wooden base.

"I see you've found our new arrival," said the shop owner. An air of mystery clung to her, though a warm smile lit her eyes.

"It's lovely," Laura murmured. On impulse, she decided she had to have the piece as a memento of her new life in Mistletoe. "I'll take it."

After Laura paid for her latest treasure, the shop owner bent over the counter, brushed silver strands of hair back into her chignon, and wrapped the snow globe in large sheets of paper. "Are you enjoying Mistletoe?"

"I am. Actually, I just moved here."

"How nice! Welcome to Mistletoe." She extended her hand. "I'm Jessica."

"Laura."

Jessica's eyes crinkled at the corners as she handed the bag to Laura. "You know, this is a very special snow globe."

"Is it? How so?"

"It's got a touch of Christmas magic in it. I'm told it chooses its owners. It seems it chose you."

Laura enjoyed the old woman's sales puffery, but she couldn't resist saying, "Probably because I'm willing to spend ninety dollars on it." She chuckled.

Jessica regarded Laura as though sizing her up. "Perhaps."

Laura smiled. "Well, this owner's on a budget. But I allow myself one special Christmas decoration each year. And this year, I think this will be it." The snow globe was actually over her budget, but if it doubled as a housewarming gift, she could justify the purchase.

"It's a small price to pay for a little Christmas magic."

"I've outgrown Christmas magic, but I do love a snow globe."

"Christmas magic never outgrows people. It's a shame it's the other way around."

The shop owner was good; she would give her that. But the woman had a point, one that made Laura wistful. "It's part of growing up." After exchanging cordial holiday wishes with the woman, Laura left the shop.

Outside, snowflakes danced in the breeze as she strolled through the square, clutching her magical snow globe. The Christmas village inside, with a gentle snowfall, filled her with wistful, childlike joy. It would serve as a tangible reminder of why she'd chosen to move there. The town's charm infused every corner of Mistletoe. She would have that same feeling inside her home, to remind her of the quaint small-town appeal that had motivated her to relocate to Mistletoe. It was the start of her wonderful new life.

Once home, she wasted no time unpacking the

Christmas decorations and placing them around her cozy living room. Piles of boxes still surrounded her, but she had a pot of pine branches near the window to scent the room with holiday cheer. Red and green stockings hung from her fireplace, fairy lights adorned every doorway, and a festive wreath decked the chimney. She might not have finished unpacking, but Laura was ready to enjoy Christmas in all its glory.

With a contented sigh, she sank into an armchair and gazed around as warmth flooded her chest. The place already felt like home.

THE NEXT MORNING dawned bright and clear, with blades of sunlight cutting through the trees and casting shadows across the bright snow. Laura hummed along to "White Christmas" as she made coffee, anticipation quickening her pulse.

She had just taken the first bite of her toast when her phone rang and displayed her old office phone number. She scowled and answered with a short greeting.

"Laura." Fran's poorly concealed relief rushed out. "I'm sorry to bother you, but we can't locate the final draft of the quarterly report for the meeting in an hour."

Laura shut her eyes and took a moment then tried not to sound too dismayed. "It's on our shared drive in the cloud. I even copied Allison and Jason on it." Same old Fran—flummoxed by technology.

"I guess I must've looked in the wrong folder or something."

"It's the one marked Quarterly Reports. If you don't see it, try searching online for it."

"Oh. That's a good idea."

And an obvious one. "I'm sure Allison or Jason could help you."

"Yeah, but I hate to ask them. They always seem so put out."

"Don't let them intimidate you. It's their job," Laura replied, tight-lipped.

A heavy sigh came over the line before Fran spoke again. "Yes, I know that." Another deep sigh followed by silence reminded Laura why she'd quit her job. It was the same reason she'd chosen to move away before the holidays. She would be able to enjoy a stress-free holiday season surrounded by family without having to worry about being deluged by stress from the office. And come the new year, she would start her new job and work remotely from home.

Laura took the few moments of silence as her cue. "Have a merry Christmas!"

Fran sounded hesitant but returned happy holiday wishes and ended the call.

With a shudder, Laura went to the mantel, where she'd proudly placed her new snow globe the evening before. As she turned it over to make it snow, she let out a pleasant gasp. "It plays music!" She lifted the hinged handle and turned it a few times. Then she set it down and watched the snow swirl as it played "Have Yourself a Merry Little Christmas."

"That's funny. I don't remember that house looking that much like mine, except my house doesn't have an impressively muscular guy at the door. No surprise there."

Upon further examination, she decided he looked like Michelangelo's David in L.L. Bean clothes. "If you showed up at my door, I wouldn't turn you away."

It had been a long time since she'd had a man in her life—so long that she had to think back and count. Three years. She had reached a point where it was easier to give up than to suffer through any more dates and relationships that didn't work out. Her sister was right about two things: she had terrible taste in men, and she was undatable. Once she'd accepted those two items as facts, it relieved all the pressure.

With a rueful smile, Laura set down the snow globe and peered at her little lumberjack. "Why can't Santa drop a hot guy like you down my chimney?" As if in reply, the snow globe shimmered in the morning sunlight. Laura laughed and headed for the kitchen to refill her coffee.

TWO

BY MIDAFTERNOON, Laura was carrying one of the last boxes out of the moving pod when thunder rumbled from the east. A cold gust of wind swept strands of hair over her face, sending a shiver down her spine. As the brilliant sunshine gave way to a deluge, she closed the pod doors and scurried inside. With a frustrated sigh, she shook the water out of her hair and peered out the window. The once sparkling harbor was now tempest-tossed, with silver lightning illuminating the churning waves with each clap of thunder.

Suddenly, another sound pricked her ears—dripping water. Pivoting, Laura discovered a slow drip from the ceiling. Scanning the stacks of identically sized and symmetrically arranged boxes yet to be unpacked, she located the pots, pans, and large mixing bowls. Her sister had always laughed at her painstaking organization, but thanks to thorough labeling, she quickly retrieved a large pot. As she hurried to place it under the leak before it became a stream, she grumbled, "How do you like your charming Christmas cottage with its quaint leaking roof?" That wasn't part of the plan.

With the leak getting worse, she had to do something. When things went wrong in her apartment, she'd always called the super, but there was no super there. What she needed was a handyman, so she pulled out her phone and searched online. *There's only one handyman listed?* Her brow furrowed at the results. *Well, you wanted small-town living.*

After dialing the number, she was surprised when, instead of voicemail, she got a brusque "Hello?"

"Hello! Is this Farley Cooper?"

"Who's calling?"

"Laura. Laura Everly."

"Everly... Not familiar with the name. Where are you?"

"At 45 Chestnut Lane. I just moved here."

"Oh, right. The little red house?"

Placing another pot under a fresh leak, Laura said, "Sorry, but can we talk later? Right now, I've got a waterfall forming in my living room."

A pause followed before the husky, masculine voice replied confidently, "I'm on my way."

"Really?"

"That's what I said."

"Great!"

Laura hastily added a large mixing bowl as another leak spouted, only to have a sudden downpour of water drench her completely. Soon, drywall fragments fell on her with the force of a storm surge, leaving her hair sopping. She cried out then tamped down her emotions. She had to think clearly. A puddle was forming and working its way to her neatly stacked boxes. Frantic, she threw down a kitchen towel and hurried to move the boxes across the room. Laura prided herself on maintaining control through assiduous planning and organization, but her entire world was falling apart.

A brisk knock snapped her out of her daze. As she opened the door, a gust of wind blew an icy mist at her face, blinding her for a moment. When she was able to focus again, instead of finding the older man she'd pictured—one with a worn face and worn work clothes—Laura found herself face-to-face with a man in his early thirties with sandy-blond hair and piercing blue eyes.

His chiseled features and broad shoulders projected a sense of quiet authority as he assumed an expectant stance on her doorstep. He was ruggedly handsome, with a day's worth of stubble gracing his jaw. His flannel shirt clung to his muscular arms. Laura guessed he was over six feet tall by the way he towered over her.

When she didn't immediately speak, his intense eyes narrowed slightly with impatience. "I'm Cooper. You called me?" he said in a deep voice.

Laura swallowed. "Yes, Farley Cooper," she managed to get out, feeling suddenly flustered. Stepping aside, she invited him in.

He gave a terse nod, his expression unreadable. "Everyone calls me Cooper."

Unsettled, she stared and repeated, "Cooper."

He peered at her with a hint of amusement in his eyes. "Are you okay? Have you injured your head?" He pointed toward her hair.

She reached up with both hands and grasped a chunk of drywall still dangling from the side of her head. "Yeah, I'm fine. But the ceiling... Well, see for yourself." He brushed past her and walked across the room. As she followed, Laura asked, "How did you get here so quickly?"

"I live two blocks over."

Without further pleasantries, he examined the damage. Meanwhile, she watched the play of muscles across his broad back as he reached up to the ceiling.

After a quick inspection upstairs, Cooper descended the stairs briskly and went outside without a word. Laura hesitated then grabbed her jacket and slipped it on while she followed. He had an air of no-nonsense efficiency about him that left her feeling wrong-footed. She wasn't sure what to make of the enigmatic handyman, but one thing was certain: he was even better looking than the snow globe figurine that had first made her wish for him.

That's odd. But I didn't really wish, exactly. It was more of a comment. You have to rub things to make wishes come true. Except that's more of a magic lamp thing. Snow globes must be different. Hello! Have you lost your mind? 'Cause you sound kind of crazy. And you're talking to yourself!

While Cooper inspected the waterlogged ceiling, Laura forced her thoughts back to more pressing matters like her caving-in ceiling and Cooper. Who lived two blocks over. If that was an example of what she would find two blocks over, she needed to get out and explore her new neighborhood. But her new neighbor's frown brought her back to the present predicament.

Cooper shook his head. "Hold on a sec." He went upstairs, and Laura finished moving her boxes away from the water. After a brief upstairs inspection, Cooper came downstairs and went outside. Moments later, he returned and stuck his head in the door. "Can you come here and give me a hand?"

Pulling her hood up to shield her from the rain, she followed him to the side of the house. With a tarp slung over his shoulder, a nail gun in his hand, and a ladder under his arm, he lifted his eyes to the roof. "That's where your leak is. Your home inspector should've caught that."

When she stared blankly, he rolled his eyes. "You didn't get a home inspection?"

All she could offer was a helpless shrug.

He winced. "Did you think your down payment and dreams were enough?"

"No! I just thought I'd make it through the night without the roof caving in. But thanks for the warm welcome and encouraging words." Sure, he was hot, but that didn't make up for his disposition, which was downright annoying and so disappointing.

He looked straight at her with those deep-blue eyes, and she almost forgot not to like him. She couldn't read his expression but decided she didn't care.

"Hold this," he said. After repositioning her hands and cautioning her to keep the ladder steady, he climbed up onto the roof.

While Laura held the ladder, she couldn't help but notice his physique as he climbed up, tarp in tow. Hmm. Still, having a hot body didn't give him the license to be condescending. But he was up on her roof, fixing her leak in the rain. She couldn't fault him for that. Once he'd secured the tarp, Cooper descended.

Having decided that the less said, the better, Laura waited while he pulled down the ladder.

"Let me put this away, and I'll meet you inside."

Laura stood at the door, and Cooper grabbed a wet vac from his truck. Once inside, he said, "It's not looking good, but I've covered the leak. I'll go clean upstairs."

An hour later, he'd vacuumed up the standing water in her upstairs bathroom. "Your bathroom is a gut job, but the damage down here is minimal—just the ceiling, really. I'll have to rent a couple of industrial fans and dehumidifiers to dry this out before I can begin the repairs. It'll take about two weeks to dry and another couple of weeks to do the repairs."

"But... Christmas is in three weeks." Laura's dreams of a picture-perfect Christmas appeared rather soggy.

"Do you want mold growing inside your walls?"

Laura frowned. "Well, no, but..."

He repeated. "Two weeks."

The phrase echoed in Laura's mind.

"I'll bring the fans tomorrow," Cooper promised.

"Wait. That sounds like a pretty big job. I think I should get a second opinion."

Cooper leveled a stare at her, along with that unreadable expression she was growing used to. When he said nothing for several seconds, Laura searched for words to end the unsettling silence.

Before she could speak, he said, "Suit yourself." With that, he turned and picked up his wet vacuum.

"Wait. How much do I owe you?"

"We'll sort that out later."

"Later... when?"

"When you've gotten your second opinion."

That sounded awfully presumptuous, but she held her tongue. "All right."

Cooper paused before climbing into his truck. "It's your lucky day. The rain has stopped."

"Yeah. Lucky me." She sulked as he pulled out of the driveway.

THE SUN WAS SETTING over the town square, gilding the rooftops and church spire with golden light as Laura stepped out of the car. The rain damage might have dampened her spirits, but she would be back on track soon. She just needed advice from the only person in town that she knew.

The door to the antiques shop struck the small overhead bell, prompting Jessica to emerge from a room in the back. "Laura, hello!"

"Hi, Jessica." Laura smiled. "I wonder if I could ask for your advice. You're the only person I know here in town. I need a handyman—someone who can repair some rain damage to my roof and ceiling."

"Oh, I'm sorry to hear that."

Laura shrugged. "Thanks. I'm afraid it's going to put a dent in my Christmas budget. Can you recommend anyone?"

Without hesitation, Jessica said, "Farley Cooper."

"That was quick. Is he really that good?"

Jessica smiled. "He is. He's also the only

handyman in town. I suppose you could try out of town, but nobody does. We like to support our local businesses."

"Actually, he stopped by already to assess the damage. I just didn't know whether I could trust him."

A twinkle came to Jessica's eyes. "You can trust him."

Still unconvinced, Laura said, "Oh. Hmm. I just got a hard-to-work-with vibe from him."

"Who, Cooper?" She blew air through her lips. "I've known Cooper since he was in diapers. He was an adorable baby." She regarded Laura with twinkling eyes. "He's not hard to look at now, either."

Laura smiled politely, but his looks weren't her biggest concern. "And you're sure he's up to the job?"

"Absolutely."

"Well, that's good to hear. I guess I'll go give him a call." With her phone to her ear, Laura left.

That time, Laura got Cooper's voicemail. "Cooper, it's Laura—Laura Everly. At 45 Chestnut Lane. Can you call me back?"

After grabbing a couple of things from the grocery store and stopping for gas, Laura headed home.

She pulled into her driveway to find Cooper leaning on his truck, arms folded. As soon as Laura got out of her car, he said, "I brought the fans and dehumidifiers. Let's get to work."

"But I haven't hired you yet."

With a shrug, he said, "You just called."

"Yeah, but—"

"How did your second opinion work out?"

"Jessica at the antiques shop said you're the best person for the job."

His confident smirk annoyed her, but she reminded herself that she wasn't hiring him for his congeniality. He was fixing her house. "Okay. You're hired."

THREE

AFTER A NIGHT of trying to sleep to the sounds of industrial fans and dehumidifiers and a full day of unpacking boxes, Laura needed a break, so she headed to town. A few people strolled down the sidewalks, ducking into shops or heading home after a day of work or errands. A balsam fir tree towered over the town square, filling the air—and her heart—with the essence of Christmas. From the bakery came an aroma of cinnamon and cloves, so she doubled back and went inside to pick up some holiday treats.

Twilight was falling as she headed home with renewed hope for a magical Christmas—even if it wouldn't look that way inside her house for the next week or two. Compared to her former home with city traffic and her stress at having to chase promotions, she could endure a couple of weeks of repairs.

The first stars were winking into view when Laura unlocked the front door, stepped inside, and took off her coat. If she ignored the fans and the damaged corner, the house already seemed cozy and lived in. Even her apartment furnishings and decorations looked better there. *All I need is some music.*

Laura turned on the gas fireplace and lifted the snow globe. The miniature village caught the firelight and glowed as she wound the key. Tinkling music filled the room with holiday cheer as she sank onto the sofa and sighed. Her cottage might be torn apart at the moment, but her walk through the village had renewed her love for her new community and strengthened her resolve to make it work, home repairs or not. If she had any doubt, she needed only to gaze at her snow globe, a symbol of her new beginning.

THE MORNING SUN filtered through the sheer curtains and shed soft light on the scattered boxes and unpacked clothing that filled Laura's new bedroom. She stretched her arms overhead and rose to tackle a new day of unpacking.

As she fell into a rhythm of tearing tape and rustling paper, her phone vibrated on the windowsill. Cooper's name appeared on the screen. "Hi, Cooper!"

"Morning. I'm calling to give you a heads-up. I'll be over in about twenty minutes to work on your roof."

"Okay. See you then." As she ended the call, Laura stared at the half-emptied box before her. Cooper's call had stirred up a swirl of emotions she couldn't quite pin down. Ever since she'd brought home that snow globe, an irrational part of her wondered if it really did have the power to make wishes come true. After all, she had jokingly wished for a man like the one in the figurine, and soon after, Cooper showed up to fix her roof. Because stuff like that happened all the time. No, enchanted snow globes were the stuff of fairy tales, not real life.

And yet, doubt nagged at the corners of her mind. The roof was an inconvenience, but it had brought Cooper into her life, a man who both intrigued and flustered her more than she cared to admit. He was also a man who bore an uncanny resemblance to the man in her snow globe. Who knew she could wish in such vivid detail? Because Cooper was her idea of perfection.

Laura shook her head, laughing softly to herself. "Girl, you are losing your mind." The whimsy of the holiday season was playing tricks on her logical brain. She had to stop fixating on the snow globe and focus on what was real—unpacking, enjoying the holidays, then starting the new year with a new job.

With renewed determination, Laura picked up

another box and resumed unpacking. But a lingering seed of doubt over the snow globe's connection remained in the back of her mind, refusing to be ignored.

Three boxes later, she paused and glanced toward the kitchen. "I think I've earned some caffeine." She headed to the kitchen to put the kettle on. While instant coffee was a poor substitute for the real thing, it would have to suffice. She breathed in the rich, comforting aroma which filled the room as she stirred the granules into the steaming water. Nestling the warm mug close to her chest, Laura leaned against the rough stones of the fireplace, enjoying its warmth.

She took a sip and grimaced. "What I wouldn't give for a decent cup of coffee!" An inexplicable shiver rippled over her skin. From the mantel, the snow globe flickered briefly, its miniature world ignited by a fleeting, magical spark. She shook her head. *It's just the flickering firelight playing tricks with my vision.*

A firm knock at her door startled her. She set down her mug and went to answer the door. There stood Cooper holding a cardboard tray containing two cups of steaming coffee and a white box tied with string. Whatever it contained smelled delicious.

"I had a craving for some coffee and muffins from the bakery in town, so I brought extras." His blue eyes made contact for a fleeting moment then flickered away.

"Wow!" Laura exclaimed, her face lighting up with genuine gratitude. "You know, I was just wishing for coffee, and then you showed up."

"It's just coffee," he replied as though she were making too much of a fuss.

"And a muffin!" she added enthusiastically. She wasn't sure, but she thought she saw a glimmer of light in Cooper's eyes and the slightest hint of a smile.

"Have a seat," she said warmly, gesturing for him to join her by the fireplace. "You can't hammer roof tiles, drink coffee, and eat a muffin at the same time."

"Oh, believe me, I've done it—although not very well."

They settled into the comfortable armchairs, angled to face the crackling fire. Laura caught sight of the snow globe and thought back on the last several minutes. She'd wished for decent coffee, then Cooper showed up with the best coffee in town. It had to be a coincidence, except she couldn't quite dismiss it so easily. She recalled the shop owner's words. "It's got a touch of Christmas magic in it." *It couldn't really, though. Could it?* The snow globe flickered as if in reply. Unsettled, Laura looked out the window, hoping to find an explanation. *It was a reflection. That's all.*

As they sipped from their mugs, Laura searched for a distraction. "So, you don't go by your first name?"

"No, it's always been Cooper. The only one who dares call me Farley is my mother."

"It's an unusual name."

"Yeah, well, my mom loves old movies, so she named me after a movie actor." He shrugged helplessly, like a man long since resigned to a name he clearly wasn't fond of. "So, why Mistletoe?"

She got the impression he wasn't so much interested in that answer as he was in easing the awkwardness, which seemed to fill the air like an unpleasant static charge. But she answered for the same reason he'd asked. "I used to come here on day trips from the city, and it always made me feel so... I don't know, happy. Then I'd go back to the job that I hated and the stress of the city. One day I asked myself why, and I didn't have an answer. So I set a goal to move here. And here I am."

After she said it, she realized how she must sound to him, and she felt the need to clarify. "It's not that I'm flighty. I spent years doing all the things you're supposed to do—working long hours, chasing promotions, trying to say and do the right things to succeed. And I guess I burned out. It just wasn't for me." She looked over at him and was surprised by what she saw.

Cooper's eyes softened, and Laura felt something in her heart stir as he said, "I know what you mean."

"Really?" That was a side of him she hadn't seen —human.

He looked off into the distance then continued. "When I got out of college, I worked at a bank. Yeah, I guess you wouldn't have expected that from me." His scowl turned into a smirk as his hand brushed through his untamed mop of dark-blond hair.

"Wow."

He scowled. "Wow what?"

Laura tried not to look defensive. "Oh, nothing. I just... You're right. Banker wouldn't have been my first thought."

His voice was laced with self-mockery. "I'll take that as a compliment."

Laura suppressed a smile. She hadn't meant it as one, although she hadn't meant it as an insult either. "So, you worked at the bank here in town?"

He narrowed his eyes. "No, Bangor. There's nothing wrong with it. It just wasn't the right place for me. So I quit the bank and came home." He turned to her. "We have that in common."

Those eyes of his were intense, as was her reaction. It was only a moment, but it had caught her off guard.

Laura understood why he'd come home. It was the same reason she'd moved there.

"My favorite time here is Christmas. I timed my move so I'd be here by Christmas."

"This place is magic during the holidays."

She tried not to sound too surprised. "You don't seem like the Christmassy type."

He laughed lightly. "Well, you can't judge a book by its cover, now can you?"

"Apparently not."

The warm light never left his eyes as they locked gazes for a moment—a moment that caught them both off guard but slowly melted away any lingering hesitation between them.

She tried to rally. "I imagine that after living in Mistletoe, you'd find that anywhere else paled in comparison."

"Yeah," he replied as a warm light came to his eyes. "Mistletoe is an experience. At Christmas, the town really comes together."

Laura sighed softly, her mind drifting to the enchantment of her first holiday season in a place where the streets would come alive with twinkling lights and vibrant merriment during December.

For a moment, the room fell into a hushed stillness with only the gentle crackle of logs in the fireplace in the air. Laura studied Cooper's face and those unsettling eyes. A sense of limitless possibilities seemed to charge the surrounding air.

Cooper exhaled and stood. "I should probably get started on that roof."

"Of course," Laura replied, trying to look nonchalant. "Thanks for the coffee and muffins. They were delicious."

Cooper dismissed her thanks with a smirk before

turning to leave. As the door closed behind him, Laura wondered about him. She couldn't figure him out except for one undeniable truth—that tall, athletic frame and disheveled dark-blond hair made for a very good look.

FOUR

LAURA CRADLED her morning coffee mug as she
studied her miniature snow globe house. All the tiny
houses in her snow globe village had Christmas trees
in their windows. Except hers. Her house was
missing a Christmas tree. Morning sunlight streamed
through the window to the mantel, giving the snow
globe a glimmering aura.

"Look at us," Laura mused aloud as she surveyed
the room. "We're the only house without a Christmas
tree." She glanced out the window at the sunny day
then sighed. "I wish..." But as she eyed the boxes still
left to unpack, she said, "No. Unpacking now,
Christmas tree shopping later."

The snow globe pulsed with light.

Laura turned sharply and stared. She lifted the
globe and turned it over to look at the bottom. No, there
was no switch. The globe didn't light up. Except it just

had. Shaking her head, she decided there had to be a logical explanation. A car probably drove by with some chrome that reflected the sun on the snow globe. She wondered how much chrome trim was on cars anymore. It could have been an old car or truck. Whatever it was, it was gone, and the snow globe looked perfectly normal. She set it down and dug into a large cardboard box.

But Christmas tree thoughts stirred her inner childlike anticipation of the magic of the season. Perhaps it was the upheaval of the ongoing repair work, but the thought fixed itself in her mind that her house would not be a home without a proper Christmas tree. It would be an unpacked house, but it wouldn't feel like home. Despite a long list of practical tasks to complete, she bumped the Christmas tree to the top of the list. All she needed was a Christmas tree farm.

She pulled out her phone to search for one, but the rumble of Cooper's old red pickup truck drew her attention outside. He pulled into her driveway, and he was dressed in a flannel shirt and jeans. He looked every bit the rugged outdoorsman. As he began unloading roofing supplies from the truck bed, he caught sight of her standing by the window. Their eyes met, but there was no wave or smile, so Laura stepped back from the window. Did he do that on purpose, or was it a gift—making her feel so disconcerted? Doing her best to shake off the feeling, she grabbed her coat and keys and headed outside. The crisp winter air was refreshing.

"Cooper," she called out as she neared the truck. "Do you know if there's a Christmas tree farm in the area? My house needs a tree."

"Yeah," he replied, wiping his hands on a rag before tucking it into his back pocket. "There's a great one a few miles down the road." He pointed toward the edge of town. "Head down Main Street, take a left onto Maple, and keep driving a couple of miles. Just follow the signs. You can't miss it."

"Thanks!" She brightened with anticipation. But when she turned the key in the ignition, nothing happened. She tried it again. And again. It refused to start. First the roof, then her car. With a frustrated sigh, she stormed out of the car and gave the tire a kick.

"What did that tire do to you?" Cooper's voice was tinged with humor as he approached her.

"It's an accessory to the crime. My car won't start." Laura shook her head, then a thought came to mind. "What do you know about cars?"

"I know how to call a mechanic."

Her shoulders slumped. "Oh. I guess today's not my Christmas tree day after all."

"I'll tell you what." Cooper scratched his head thoughtfully. "I was planning on going later this week to get one for my mom." He shrugged. "But today's just as good. We could make a morning of it if you'd like."

Laura wasn't sure how to react. She had to have misunderstood because it almost appeared he was being nice. "Really?"

Squinting, he peered at her as though she were a little off. "Yeah."

He'd done it to her again—made her feel unsure of herself. She stammered. "Well, I just... I mean, are you sure it's not too much trouble?"

"If it was any trouble, I wouldn't have offered."

"I know, but I don't want to impose."

He frowned. "Just say thank you and get in the truck."

"But my car..."

"I know the tow guy."

"Of course you do."

"I'll call him." He paused, raising an eyebrow. "Unless you'd rather get a second opinion."

Laura supposed she deserved that. "No, I trust your judgment."

He leaned back, feigning surprise. "Well, that's progress."

She wasn't sure whether he was being sarcastic or truly annoyed, but to her relief, his lips curved up at one corner as he pulled out his phone. A quick conversation later, he shoved the phone back into his pocket. "All settled. Just leave it unlocked with the keys on the car seat."

Pleased but confused, Laura asked, "But where's he going to take it?"

His eyes lit up with amusement. "His garage is just off Main Street in town. He'll call us once he knows what needs to be done."

"Okay." She still couldn't believe how easy that was.

"So." Cooper lifted his eyebrows. "To the tree farm?"

The thought restored her good mood. "To the tree farm!"

The journey to the farm was filled with as comfortable a silence as she'd known with the guy. The only sounds were the hum of the truck's engine and the soft Christmas carols playing on the radio. Laura studied Cooper in the dim light. The lines of concentration on his face as he navigated the icy roads, the way his hands skillfully controlled the steering wheel, and the quiet strength that, despite everything she'd experienced so far, drew her in.

A thin blanket of fresh snow covered the ground, adding to the magical charm of the Christmas tree farm setting. Bundled up in her parka, Laura found her heart fluttering with anticipation.

As they strolled along the parking area of the driveway, rows of evergreens waited in the distance. The scent of pine and damp earth filled the air, mingling with the soft crunch of snow beneath their boots. Inside the gate, evergreens lined the walkway, filling Laura with a surge of delight. There were so many trees, each one more perfect than the last. She couldn't help reaching out to touch the soft needles.

"First time at a tree farm?" Cooper asked, his eyes twinkling with amusement.

Laura nodded, self-conscious. "It is." With a sheepish grin, she admitted, "I'm a city girl."

"We'll have to fix that." When he grinned, his blue eyes lit up. But his laughter faded to quiet contentment as they entered the barn. Holiday lights wrapped around the rustic beams lent a soft glow to the space.

"Here." Laura handed Cooper a mug of steaming cocoa.

"Thanks," he replied, taking a cautious sip of the rich, velvety liquid. "So, tell me about your life before you moved to Mistletoe."

Laura hesitated, her eyes drawn to the dancing flames of a nearby lantern. Cooper didn't make it easy to open up to him, yet the same off-putting honesty that so often repelled her had made her trust him. Still, sharing her story meant revealing her vulnerabilities—something she hadn't done in a very long time.

"Before I came here, I had a high-stress job in the city," she began, her voice barely above a whisper. "It was all-consuming. My life was nothing but work, deadlines, and never-ending demands—all of which I fulfilled while projecting an air of confidence. I had everything under control—on the outside. Inside?"

Laura let out a humorless chuckle. "I barely recognized myself anymore. That's when I decided it was time for a change."

As she spoke, Laura saw understanding in Cooper's eyes. His gaze held no judgment, only empathy. That was something she hadn't expected.

"I get it." His voice resonated with sincerity. "I tried big-city life—for a year—but it wasn't for me. Small towns aren't for everyone, but I wouldn't live anywhere else."

Laura smiled. "I agree. Maybe it's too early to tell, but I think I'll be happy here."

Cooper's blue eyes filled with warmth. "It looks like you're well on your way to doing just that."

Laura's heart swelled with hope. As she took a sip of her cocoa in the quaint barn and in the company of the intriguing Farley Cooper, she decided her life was trending upward.

Cooper raised his mug in a toast. "Here's to new beginnings."

"New beginnings," she echoed.

As they ventured deeper into the farm, Laura found herself captivated by the sight of families browsing through the trees as well as the sounds of laughter and shouts of delight echoing through the frost-tipped pines. The atmosphere was infectious.

"Which one do you think would be perfect for my living room?" she mused aloud, studying the trees with an artist's eye.

Cooper tilted his head as if considering the question. "Hmm, I think that one looks right." He pointed at a full but slightly asymmetrical tree. "It's a little quirky, like you."

Laura cast a sideways glance at him, busily brushing snow off the branches while trying not to think about what he'd meant by that. "Quirky?"

"In a good way." His eyes revealed a hint of amusement.

Laura pondered the good ways one could be quirky while she considered the tree. "Okay. This is the one."

As they stood in the clearing, surrounded by towering evergreens and a gentle snowfall, Laura glanced at the saw Cooper held, its teeth glinting in the soft light that filtered through the trees. "I'm glad you're here. I didn't realize you have to cut your own tree."

Cooper smirked. "It's a saw. Anyone can do it." He stopped sawing and turned to scrutinize her. "Even you."

Laura wrinkled her face. "I'm not saying I couldn't if I wanted to, but..."

Cooper raised an eyebrow and handed her the saw. "Here."

"What?" He couldn't be serious. He moved the saw closer as if she didn't know he expected her to take it. She knew. She just wasn't sure that she wanted to do it. "Unfortunately, I didn't wear my lumberjack outfit, so..." She shrugged helplessly, but it failed to dissuade him.

"Laura." He was serious. "Come on. You can do it."

Her pulse raced as she stared at the saw. The snow crunched beneath her boots as she shifted her weight, fully aware of how far out of her element she'd inadvertently ventured. But Cooper did not look amused. Something within her stirred. She had to rise to the challenge. Although she wanted to attribute that to her competitive nature, she genuinely cared about Cooper's opinion. She could not let the moment pass without trying.

"All right," she murmured, taking a deep breath and gripping the saw tightly. She nodded as she bolstered herself. "Okay."

Rolling her eyes in surrender, Laura took his hand and followed him to crouch at the base of the tree. As she knelt on the ground, she grabbed hold of the tree bark and breathed in the sharp scent of pine.

"Okay," Cooper began, his voice steady and patient as he explained the basics of sawing, demonstrating on the tree he'd selected for his mother. "You want to make sure you have a firm grip on the handle, then make your cut parallel to the ground. That's it. Just move the saw back and forth."

"Right. Back and forth. Got it," Laura interrupted.

Cooper chuckled, dusting off his jeans before stepping back to give her room to work.

As she grasped the saw tightly, Laura took a deep breath and began. The blade snagged on the wood several times, but she refused to let her frustration get the better of her. Instead, she focused on her breath and the satisfying sound of the saw cutting through the wood. Her muscles strained with each pass, but she was determined to succeed.

Cooper grabbed the top of the tree and pulled on the opposite side from the cut. "That's it. You've got it."

She couldn't tell whether he sounded amused or impressed, but it was oddly reassuring. As the saw shuddered through the last bits of tree trunk, the tree fell to the ground with a soft thud. With a rush of exuberance, Laura leaped to her feet.

"Ha! I did it!" She hopped up and down then did a victory dance. Then she spied Cooper staring at her with a teasing glint in his eyes.

"Sorry! I got a little carried away," she stammered as a flush crept up her cheeks.

"There's no need to apologize. It's the lumberjack way—the tree-cutting victory dance," Cooper assured her with a spark of amusement.

She narrowed her eyes and folded her arms. "Really? Let's see yours."

"Oh, I did it. You must not have been looking."

Laura slowly nodded. "Well, that's just a shame."

"Isn't it?" Then he asked, "You know what's even more fun than cutting down trees?"

"Taking them back to the truck?"

"You're catching on, city girl."

"Yay." Laura grinned and began dragging her small tree while Cooper hoisted his mother's larger tree onto his shoulder.

FIVE

Once back at the pickup, Cooper secured the trees in the bed. They were about to get into the truck when his phone rang. He spoke briefly before turning to Laura with a smile.

"My mom just invited us for dinner," he informed her. "She wants to thank you for helping pick out her tree."

Minutes later, they pulled into the driveway of a modest house on the outskirts of town. Maggie, Cooper's mother, welcomed them. She had the same warm blue eyes as her son.

"You must be Laura," she said, her voice full of warmth. "I'm so glad you're here."

"Thank you for inviting me, Mrs. Cooper."

"You're so welcome, and please call me Maggie."

As Laura followed Cooper inside the charming cottage, the scent of cinnamon and pine wafted through the air, mingling with the faint crackling of logs in the fireplace.

"Cooper, let's see that tree." While Cooper secured the tree, his mother filled the tree stand with water, and Laura directed Cooper until it was perfectly straight. Then they all stood back and surveyed their work.

"Cooper, it's perfect." Maggie gave her son a hug then said, "You two sit down. Dinner will be ready in a couple of minutes."

"Can I give you a hand with anything?" Laura asked Maggie, rolling up her sleeves in anticipation.

"Thank you." Maggie handed her an apron. "Why don't you help me set the table?"

Cooper was close behind. "I'm not going to miss out on all this fun."

So the two of them set the table and helped Maggie get dinner served.

After they'd begun eating, Laura said, "I love your china. It's such a beautiful pattern."

"These dishes belonged to my grandmother," Maggie explained, her eyes glistening with nostalgia. "They've been in the family for generations."

"Wow," Laura murmured, feeling the weight of history in her hands. "They're gorgeous."

"Wait until you see the Christmas decorations," Cooper chimed in. He winked at Laura before disappearing into the living room.

"Can I ask you something, Maggie?" Laura ventured as they continued eating their meal.

"Of course," Maggie replied, her warm eyes encouraging Laura to go on.

"Has Cooper always been, well, so good at everything?" Foremost in her mind was his work on her house, but he'd been just as adept with the trees. He'd even taught her to saw, which she had never expected.

Maggie laughed. A rich, melodious sound filled the room. "Oh, he's had his fair share of mishaps along the way," she admitted. "But he's always been determined and resourceful."

"I imagine that's a good quality for a handyman to have."

Maggie looked slightly amused, and her eyebrows drew together. "Is that what he told you, that he's a handyman?"

Laura didn't know what to make of the question. "Well, actually, no. I needed a handyman, and he was listed online, so I called him."

"I'd say that's more of a hobby for him. He enjoys working with his hands, especially outdoors. And he likes helping people out. But he's really more of a real estate developer. Well, *developer* sounds a bit grandiose. But he's restored several houses in town. He's sold some and kept others as holiday rentals."

Laura nodded thoughtfully. "I guess that makes sense. He's managed to dovetail his hobby with business." There was another layer to the man, it turned out. The laid-back handyman had a good head for business, which took some ambition—something she would never have suspected he possessed. Combined with Cooper's apparent devotion to family, the puzzle was beginning to take shape.

When they'd finished their meal and the dishes were washed, Cooper and Laura were putting on their coats when she noticed one of the wall photos. She studied the holiday portrait of two parents and a boy who looked about ten. "Is this Cooper?"

Cooper offered a reluctant nod while his mother grinned. "That's Farley."

With a patient grin, Cooper said, "That sidewalk needs some salt. I'll be back in a minute."

Beside the family portrait was a photo of Cooper standing on a dock with the same man from the portrait. Young Cooper stood proudly holding a large fish. Laura couldn't help but smile, but her smile faded as she asked gently, "And this is Cooper's father?"

Maggie's eyes softened. "Yes. That's our last picture of him."

Cooper's resemblance to his father was strong. Laura wanted to ask about him, but Maggie's eyes grew misty, so she studied the picture instead.

A few moments passed before Maggie said, "He was a fisherman. He would leave before dawn and not return until late in the evening. We used to talk about spending more time together, but money was tight, and he needed to work. And a storm came, and the sea took him."

"Oh, Maggie. I'm so sorry."

A sad smile came and went from Maggie's face. "Cooper didn't take it well. He was only twelve. We went through a rough patch. He was angry with me, with his father, and with anyone who tried to help him. He started getting into trouble at school and got in with the wrong crowd."

That was a side of Cooper that Laura couldn't have imagined.

Maggie nodded as if recalling those days. "When he started his freshman year in high school, the coach caught him smoking under the bleachers. That afternoon, he pulled Farley out of detention, took him to the gym, and put him through some drills. He came home having signed up for football and baseball. By sophomore year, he'd earned a starting position on the varsity team." Maggie paused and took a deep breath. "That coach turned Farley's life around." She drew in a breath as though she meant to go on, but Cooper returned.

"Well, we'd better get going," Cooper said. With a hug and a kiss on the cheek for his mother, he turned and opened the door before gesturing for Laura to go first. Laura gave Maggie a hug and thanked her for dinner, then they left.

Cooper was quiet on the drive home, which gave

Laura time to reflect on the evening. He was so
different from his mother with her warmth and
welcoming manner. But in a sense, the whole evening
had been a reflection of life in Mistletoe. Life was
simple and productive without being rushed. People
mattered more than schedules, not in a corporate
work-life balance sort of way but in a way that was
deep and authentic. Not that life in the city was less
real, but in the city, Laura had always been frenzied,
stressed, or exhausted, while in Mistletoe, she could
enjoy simple moments, like sitting in the home where
Cooper grew up. Despite the struggles, it was a home
full of love and the magic of Christmas.

SIX

Laura sat sipping coffee in her favorite overstuffed chair and stared at the flames in her fireplace, recalling the previous evening. *So, Cooper has a mother!* She laughed to herself. Over the course of the evening, she'd caught glimpses of the man behind the gruff, aloof persona he showed to the world. He was good to his mother. She wasn't sure why that surprised her. He'd never struck her as unkind, just efficient with his warmth.

Her last boyfriend had routinely ignored his mother's phone calls, so Laura had grown to expect that from him and perhaps from men in general. In time, her boyfriend had ignored her in person, as well. He was busy. His work as a CPA was demanding, so Laura had grown used to expecting less of his time. Her own work as an accountant kept her busy enough. They worked at the same firm, which was where they'd both met. Looking back, she realized the most they had in common was a desire for convenience. When he found someone even more convenient, he left Laura behind.

What brought that up? That was three years ago. Besides, Cooper is nothing like Alan. It's time to let go.

She thought she had, but getting rejected by her boyfriend had been enough to sour her on seeking another relationship. However, she wondered whether that had contributed to her desire to transform her life. *Maybe it's time to get out there and start dating again.*

Laura got up and went to her snow globe. In the short time she'd had it, it had become a symbol of her new life. She gazed at the miniature Christmas village inside and absently wandered back to her chair, snow globe in hand.

Until it wasn't.

Laura tripped over the ottoman and watched the snow globe slip from her fingers and fly in an arc to the overstuffed chair, where it bounced off the back and landed on the seat cushion. Heart racing, she stood staring, catching her breath.

It's okay. Nothing's broken. It's fine. Breathe.

With great care, she returned the snow globe to the safety of its home on the mantel. As she stood processing what had just happened, her phone rang, jolting her from her state of shock. It was Cooper.

Her heart skipped a beat at the sound of his voice

—probably some residual adrenaline from her snow globe's near miss.

"Your car's ready."

"Great!" She thought back on their garage conversation. Had he even told her the exact location? "You said it's off Main Street, right?"

"I can give you a ride."

She calculated how long it would take to walk there, although she still didn't know precisely where it was. Before she could ask, he said, "I'll be there in ten minutes."

Laura said, "If you'll tell me where it is, I could probably walk."

"See you then. Bye."

But... Why did he do that? She couldn't be annoyed. He was doing her a favor. She just wished she didn't always feel like they existed in different cosmic dimensions.

She had her hand on a fleece jacket when she glanced outside and saw what looked like an ominous storm on the way. Dark clouds approached from the distance, while dead leaves swirled about. Leaving the fleece on its wall hook, she went to the closet and pulled out her parka. With a mixture of relief and apprehension, she went to the garage to make sure there was room for the car, then she returned to her door and propped a snow shovel beside it. Bad weather was on the way. If it brought snow, she would be prepared. She had just pulled out her phone to look at the weather forecast when Cooper pulled into the driveway.

As she climbed into his truck, she thanked him for the ride.

He smirked. "Have you looked at the weather report?"

"No, not yet."

"There's a storm out at sea that unexpectedly changed course and is headed our way."

"Oh."

"I couldn't leave a city girl wandering through town in a snowstorm."

City girl? She turned and drew in a deep breath, about to unleash her opinion of what he could do with his city girl comment and his country boy attitude, when he turned and flashed a broad smile that completely disarmed her. That smile combined with the specks of light in his brilliant blue eyes left her dumbstruck. She settled on a feeble frown, which, judging from the slight motion of his chest, drew a silent laugh. At least he had the good sense to suppress it.

After two full blocks of silence, Cooper brought up the topic of paint color for the bathroom he was repairing. "You'll want new paint and new floor tiles, but they'll have to blend in with the existing shower."

"Okay." At the moment, she couldn't envision what all that would mean.

As if reading her mind, Cooper said, "Do some

research online, or go old-school and look at some magazine pictures. When you find a few things you like, show them to me as soon as possible. That way, we can have all the materials by the time it's dried out."

"Which will be...?"

"A week. Maybe a day or two less. With any luck, we'll have you fixed up by Christmas."

"Really? That would be perfect!" She forgot every doubt, every moment of frustration she'd ever felt toward Farley Cooper. If he finished fixing her house before Christmas, she would have her perfect Christmas again.

He pulled into the garage parking lot. Laura opened her door to get out, assuming he would be on his way.

"I'll go in and introduce you."

"You really don't—"

He hopped out of the truck and closed the door behind him.

"...have to."

A guy about Cooper's age, wearing greasy overalls and wiping his hands on a shop rag, walked in from the garage. The mechanic looked up. His eyes were round, dark pools edged in lush lashes. "Hey, Coop."

"Enzo, this is Laura Everly. Laura, this is Lorenzo Rossi, but he's been Enzo since kindergarten."

"Hi. Nice to meet you." Laura tucked a tendril of hair behind her ear.

Enzo nodded. "Hi." He took her measure long enough for Cooper to narrow his gaze as he leaned against the counter and watched them.

Enzo said, "He didn't tell me you were pretty. You are, just not what I expected at all. What did he say your name was? Clara?" When both she and Cooper scowled at him, he grinned.

Laura might have shared his amusement if she hadn't been so uncomfortable at being inside a strange place with Cooper standing so close. She didn't want to ask what was going on between them, but she sensed some competitiveness.

Laura couldn't have called it a smile, but Cooper glared with a hint of amusement and went on. "She just moved into that red cottage on Chestnut."

"Oh. Where from?"

"Bangor."

With a nod, he said, "Ah, city girl."

Laura stiffened and fought back a frown. "I was a city girl—last week. This week, I'm a town girl." She gave him her professional, not-from-the-heart smile.

Enzo chuckled easily and exchanged glances with Cooper.

Laura looked at the bill then glanced up at Cooper. "I can take it from here. You must have things to do."

He said, "No, not really. Just see you safely home and go hunker down for the storm."

She wasn't sure how to take the gesture. She was so used to tolerating him it took her a moment to sort through her feelings. "You can go hunker now. If the car doesn't start, I've got Enzo here to complain to."

Enzo smiled then folded his arms and stared at Cooper. Whatever secret code was passing between them, she chose to ignore it. Her car was fixed. That was all she cared about. She signed the paperwork, paid with her credit card, and happily took the keys Enzo had set on the counter.

Laura breathed a deep sigh of relief as she stepped out of the auto shop and into the snowy night. Snowflakes had begun drifting down and disappearing on the wet, shimmering pavement.

She'd been lucky to get her car back before the storm hit, but it was time to head home.

As much as she appreciated the protective way Cooper insisted on following her home, she decided she liked her independence even more. With a storm on the way, she preferred to stop at the grocery store unaccompanied. Before getting into her car, she paused and called out to Cooper. "I just remembered an errand I need to run, so I don't need you to follow. But thanks anyway."

Cooper didn't say a word, but she knew from the look on his face that he disapproved of her plan. "Are you sure?"

With a cheerful "I am," she got in her car and drove off. As she pulled away, she hoped she hadn't seemed rude. She felt guilty. Cooper had all the best intentions, but she'd grown accustomed to doing whatever she wished without supervision. She didn't like feeling dependent on anyone, especially a man she barely knew. Cooper in particular had a way of stirring up feelings, conflicting emotions that left her feeling troubled, so redrawing the boundary between them seemed like a wise thing to do.

COOPER WATCHED as Laura's car disappeared into the descending gloom, the first snowflakes of the coming storm beginning to accumulate on the ground.

"Well, Coop, looks like you got ditched," Enzo remarked, a smirk playing on his face.

Cooper grunted, shoving his hands into his pockets as the cold began to bite. "Not ditched, Enzo, released. There's a difference."

"Uh-huh, right," Enzo retorted with a chuckle. "Keep telling yourself that. You know, you're not so smooth around that one." He inclined his head in the direction Laura had disappeared.

Cooper turned to his friend, eyebrows knitted. "What's that supposed to mean?"

Enzo shrugged. "You've got a certain... twitchiness around her. Like she makes you nervous or something."

"Nervous?" Cooper echoed. "I don't do nervous."

The mechanic's hearty laugh echoed through the dimly lit garage. "Yeah, okay. So, when are you going to tell her you like her?"

Cooper sighed. "I don't—"

"You do. Trust me," Enzo interrupted him. "Man, I've known you since we were five. I can tell."

Cooper shifted his weight from foot to foot, the cold seeping through his boots. "Even if I did, it's not... I can't."

"Can't or won't?"

"Both." The word was a whisper, a confession the wind carried away before Enzo could grasp it.

Enzo's eyes narrowed. "Why?"

"You know," Cooper retorted, a bitter edge to his voice.

Enzo wrinkled his face. "No." He peered at Cooper. "Really? Still?"

Sandra, Cooper's high school sweetheart, had promised him forever but left him for somebody else. Sandra, the one who'd taught him that love was nothing but a farce, a word people used to disguise their own selfish desires. If he'd trusted his instincts, he wouldn't have let Sandra in close. He'd shut down pretty well after his father died, but Sandra had worked her way into his heart. They said he was too young for true love at that age, but it felt true to him. After Sandra, Cooper got smart. He had a few girlfriends, nothing serious, because he wouldn't let anyone get close enough to hurt him. He was over her. Only walls remained to protect him—walls he couldn't tear down even for Laura.

Enzo sighed. "Cooper, Sandra was a long time ago, and she wasn't right for you. Laura's not Sandra. She's different."

Cooper smirked. "How do you know? You just met her."

Enzo leveled a knowing look at Cooper. "I don't need to know her. It's the look on your face."

Cooper shook his head. "She's a stranger. She's just passing through."

"I thought she bought a house here. That sounds pretty permanent."

With a shrug, Cooper said, "She's just another city girl who thinks it'll be cute to live in a small town. She'll tire of it and move back. They all do."

"Do they?"

"She will."

Enzo stared in disbelief. "Or is that what you wish so you don't have to deal with feelings?"

Cooper stared in disgust. "Wow. What has marriage done to you? If you pull out a hanky and start dabbing your eyes, I'm outta here."

Enzo was the first to laugh, but Cooper joined in. Enzo brushed the hair from his forehead with the back of his wrist. "Sorry, man. The wife made me go to a couples' retreat."

Full of pity, Cooper said, "Aw, man."

"But enough about me. About this Laura..."

"She has a life and a career. She doesn't need complications."

"Just one complication. She looks like she can take it."

Cooper stared into the distance. "Yeah, she probably can. But I've got enough social life."

"Sure, if you count talking to your dog as social interaction."

Cooper threw a faux glare at Enzo. "Leave Duke out of this."

The two men laughed, the humor momentarily dispersing the growing cold around them. When the laughter faded, Cooper shifted the subject. "Enough about me. What about you? How's the family?"

Enzo shrugged. "Same old, same old. I'm ankle deep in toys and potty training. That didn't sound right. At least the potty training's confined to the bathroom. Well, most of the time. But I'm not going to lie. I've thought about running away and joining the circus." He chuckled.

Despite the chill, warmth spread through Cooper. Enzo's chaos sounded like the life he'd once envisioned—the kind he was reluctant to envision with Laura.

"I wouldn't trade it for anything, though," Enzo

continued, pulling Cooper from his thoughts. "They're my world."

"Yeah, I can see that," Cooper responded, the slight envy in his voice undetectable.

Just then, a gust of wind hit them, bringing with it a handful of icy snowflakes that caught them in the face. Cooper squinted against the onslaught, his heart sinking. "Time to head home. Looks like it's going to be a bad one."

Enzo followed his gaze, his smile fading. "Yeah. I hope Laura gets home okay."

Cooper turned to his truck, and his mind suddenly filled with images of Laura trying to navigate through a blizzard. "She will," he assured Enzo, not entirely sure who he was trying to convince.

As he climbed into his truck, his eyes lingered on the path Laura's car had taken, worry gnawing at his insides. But Laura was independent and stubborn; she'd proven that already. Cooper had to trust that she knew what she was doing.

With a last nod to Enzo, he drove off into the growing storm, his thoughts echoing Enzo's last words. He hoped Laura would be okay.

SEVEN

COOPER PULLED out of the garage parking lot, his truck rumbling as he headed for the grocery store. Snowflakes flew at the windshield and coated the ground in a pristine white blanket. It was nothing he hadn't seen before, so he'd committed his storm preparation list to memory: beer, chips, cookies, and frozen pizza. He chuckled to himself as he mentally arranged them in a food pyramid.

Stepping into the store, he found a few shoppers and sparse shelves. The sensible ones had already secured their supplies, leaving Cooper with a sense of solitude amidst the towering shelves. Not minding the tranquil shopping experience, he gathered his essentials and made his way to the checkout counter.

With his purchases rung up, Cooper walked out to his truck, the cold air biting at his face. The thought crossed his mind to drive by Laura's house to make sure she'd made it home safely. It was on his way if he took an alternate route. He tried to tell himself he was being overly protective, if not irrational, but he drove by anyway.

"Man, look at yourself." He laughed. However, his laughter quickly subsided when he arrived at Laura's house and found her driveway empty. Worry took hold, and he debated whether he should search for her. But then reason prevailed. He reminded himself they were practically strangers, and she had made it clear she had errands to run—alone. It wasn't his place to get involved. So, he headed home instead. As he did, he wondered if that was how stalkers got started.

He'd just popped the tab on a beer when his phone startled him with an incoming call. Panic gripped him as he answered, fearing the worst. "Laura?"

"Cooper?" Her voice sounded shaky. "I'm so sorry."

"For what? Are you okay?" His heart pounded in his chest, his worry turning into action. "Where are you?" he asked, his voice laced with concern.

"I tried to call Enzo, but there's no answer."

Cooper interrupted. "He didn't fix your car?"

"He did, but..." She heaved a sigh.

"Laura. Are you okay?"

"Yeah. A little shaken up, but—"

"Tell me what happened."

"I'm trying. The car is fine. Or at least it was until I took a corner, and another car took the opposite corner, and we both started skidding. I kind of spun around, and now I'm stuck in a ditch."

"Are you sure you're not hurt?"

"Well, my pride is a little bruised."

"Where are you?"

"Uh, I don't really know. I can only see one street sign, and it's covered with snow."

"What else do you see?"

"Uh, houses?"

Cooper exhaled. "Where were you coming from?"

"I just went to the grocery store. I was on my way home."

Cooper tried to control the anger roiling within him—not with her but with himself. He should never have let her drive off alone—except she was an adult and didn't need his permission. "Laura, I was just there. I could have picked up whatever you needed. You don't need to be driving around in that little two-wheel-drive compact of yours."

"Thanks. That's helpful."

Cooper heaved a sigh. "Sorry. Let's back up. You were on your way home from the grocery store when you turned a corner and skidded off the road. Are you on the right side or the left?"

"Left."

"Is your phone charged up?"

"Yeah."

"Good. I'm on my way there."

"Cooper?"

"What?"

"Thanks."

"No problem."

Snowflakes swirled around his truck as he navigated the treacherous roads, his thoughts consumed by the image of Laura stranded in the midst of a New England storm. Retracing the most obvious route from the grocery store, he found her car hopelessly trapped in a snow-covered ditch. Bundled up in her coat, Laura greeted him with a mixture of relief and embarrassment. Cooper offered her a reassuring smile and urged her to hop into his warm truck.

"Thank you so much for coming," she said, her voice filled with gratitude.

"It's no problem at all," Cooper replied, his concern clear. "Are you sure you're okay?"

She nodded, her eyes locking with his for a moment. "I'll be fine. I just thought, since it was only a five-minute drive, it wouldn't be a problem."

Cooper tried not to show his disagreement. "I'm just glad you're safe. As for your car, there's not much we can do now. When the storm subsides, we can see about getting it towed. Come on. Let's get you home."

Once there, Cooper insisted on walking her to the door.

Feeling annoyed yet embarrassed, she said, "I can walk to the door."

"You should put some salt on those steps."

Laura wasn't about to tell him she didn't have any. That was one of those things she'd never had to think about when she was in an apartment. She unlocked the door. "See? I'm not locked out. I'll be fine."

When he didn't feel any heat coming from the house, Cooper stepped inside. "It's freezing in here."

Unconcerned, Laura said, "Oh, that. Well, I turn the heat down when I'm gone."

"This doesn't feel like down. This feels off. You know, it's not a good idea to turn the heat completely off. In weather like this, your pipes could freeze." He went to the thermostat to turn it up.

When he stood staring intently, Laura explained, "It usually takes a few minutes for the heat to kick in."

He cast a doubtful look at her. "Nothing's kicking in. I don't hear a sound. I'll just take a look at your boiler." He headed for the stairs to the basement.

Emerging a few minutes later, he said, "The good news is your boiler isn't broken."

"See? I told you. It takes a few minutes."

Cooper winced. "When you've got oil, which you haven't."

Her look of dismay made him want to give her a sympathetic hug, but he winced as he banished the thought. Turning to practical matters, he said, "You won't be able to get an oil delivery in this storm, but let's hope for tomorrow."

Laura caught herself frowning, but she didn't want Cooper to see how upset she was. Every day seemed to bring some new way for her to fail as a homeowner. She should've done some research and found a checklist of things to stay on top of, but she was so excited about the move and the upcoming holidays that the thought had never occurred to her.

Cooper said, "You can't spend the night here."

"But I've got blankets and the gas fireplace."

"And I've got heat in the guest room." Cooper leveled her with as patient a look as he could muster.

"I couldn't. I've inconvenienced you too much already."

Cooper shrugged. "Then what's one more time?" He smiled.

Although she was still doubtful, she couldn't disagree that it was the best idea. "I'm really sorry."

"I know. So you don't have to say it again." He caught himself gazing into her wide- open eyes and glanced away. "We've got a few things to do before we can leave. Go upstairs and open your cabinet doors under the sink, then pack what you'll need overnight. While you do that, I'll open your kitchen sink cabinet doors. It's cold in here, but if we're lucky, it might be enough to keep your pipes from freezing.

While you're at it, open the tap just enough to allow a steady drip of water."

"Okay."

"While you're packing, I'll make a couple of calls to see if we can get you an oil delivery tomorrow."

THEY LOCKED up Laura's house and arrived at Cooper's minutes later. The lively patter of paws echoed from the kitchen as a German shepherd bounded and skidded around the corner, exuding infectious energy. With a playful exuberance, the dog propelled himself toward Cooper, his joyful leap culminating in an affectionate body slam. As he stood there, ears perked up and tail wagging, Laura couldn't help but notice the unmistakable twinkle of delight in Cooper's eyes.

He crouched, his hand reaching out to rub the German shepherd's neck. "Hey, Duke! How's my buddy doing?" He greeted his furry companion with genuine warmth.

Laura said hello to Duke and waited until he approached her. "He's beautiful. Is it okay to pet him?"

Cooper nodded. "Oh yeah. He likes you."

She petted Duke gently. "I like you too."

When Laura and Duke had gotten acquainted, Cooper picked up her bag. "Come on up. I'll show you your room." Once she got over how lovable Duke was, she took in the house, which was nothing like she'd expected. The whole place, or as much as she could see of it, was beautifully updated. But of course, she reminded herself that renovating homes was what he did. "Did you do all this yourself?"

With a satisfied smile, he said, "I did." Laura followed him into a room at the top of the stairs. "This is yours. Your bathroom is across the hall. You'll have it all to yourself. I've got an en suite down the hall."

"Cooper, it's gorgeous."

"And warm—its best feature this evening! I'll leave you to get settled. When you're ready, I'll have some stormy-weather provisions waiting downstairs."

"Oh, please don't go to any trouble."

He laughed. "Sorry. I didn't mean to raise your expectations. I'm talking a beer or some wine and a frozen pizza." He hastened to add, "Baked. We don't cut any corners."

Her room was a soothing combination of neutral grays and navy blue, all solid, with a nautical lamp and painting hanging over the bed. She stood for a moment, marveling at Cooper's home. Not that she'd formed a specific impression, but she'd expected something a little more haphazard in style and, well, cleanliness. But his home could have been a vacation rental. Everything appeared tastefully chosen and placed. She began to doubt her own decorating choices.

Downstairs, the inviting glow of the fireplace cast a soft light across the room. She found Cooper in the kitchen, which was once again impeccably designed with a white quartz counter and backsplash, navy-painted cabinets, and a patterned tile floor. Overall, an inviting and cozy ambiance enveloped her, offering respite from the storm raging outside, not to mention an escape from her cold home.

Cooper asked Laura what she would like to drink then poured a glass of wine and motioned for her to make herself comfortable on the couch. "I'll be there in a minute."

A half hour later, Laura rolled her eyes in feigned annoyance as Cooper beat her yet again at Scrabble. "All right, hotshot. Best two out of three?"

Cooper's eyes glinted with amusement. "Oh, it's on now. Brace yourself for a crushing defeat."

Laura laughed as Cooper reshuffled the tiles. She loved the playful side of him that emerged when they were alone. The laughter and teasing banter came easily, as did her growing feelings for him.

Later, snuggled together watching a movie, Laura stole a glance at Cooper's profile. Lit by the glow of the fireplace, he looked peaceful and content. With that bone structure, strong jaw, high cheekbones, and patrician nose, the guy didn't have a bad angle. On impulse, Laura reached out and took his hand, interlacing their fingers. Cooper turned to her, his eyes bright with affection. He lifted her hand and softly brushed his lips against her knuckles. Her heart swelled.

Laura gazed out the window at the snowflakes lit up by the outdoor spotlights. "I love the snow when it's falling—provided I am safely inside and warm."

Cooper leaned back on the couch, gazing at Laura with warmth in his eyes. "You know, when I drove past your empty driveway, I was worried."

Laura turned to him, her eyes sparkling with a mixture of gratitude and curiosity. "Thanks. I appreciate that and your hospitality. I would have spent the night wrapped in blankets and shivering by the fireplace. This is much nicer."

Their gazes locked, and his gentle, unwavering look made her heart swell. He had to have felt it too. But the stove alarm went off, and the moment was gone. Cooper returned with their pizza, and they agreed on a holiday movie. Whatever Laura had sensed in that moment was gone. When the movie was over, they headed upstairs to their respective beds.

Cooper had that searching look in his eyes again, but he kept a respectable distance. "Good night, Laura. Sleep well."

"Thanks. Good night."

As she closed the door softly behind her, she drew in a breath and exhaled. *Am I imagining this?*

I'm not even sure what this is. Electricity? Excitement? Terror? All of the above.

COOPER RETIRED to his room and sank into his chair at the window that looked out on the bay. Outside, the storm showed no sign of letting up, but inside, he had his own storm to contend with. His emotions were out of control. When had Laura crept into his heart? He'd grown used to being his own man, in charge of his feelings and enjoying a life with no emotional risks. He kept women at bay so relationships never got messy.

Messy relationships. Thoughts of Sandra, his high school sweetheart, sprang to mind. She had promised him the world only to tear his heart apart.

He still remembered the dizzy euphoria of first love, having found someone who made him believe in happy endings again after his father's tragic death. For a while, it seemed Sandra might fill the void in his heart—until the day she shattered his trust.

It was his senior year, after the homecoming game. He walked out of the locker room to find her waiting for him. It was a great game. A couple of college coaches were showing serious interest in him, so a college scholarship was almost within reach. Right there in the hallway, before dozens of people, he got down on one knee and proposed.

It had never occurred to him she might say no, but Sandra later confessed she'd never truly loved him. Utterly wrecked, he vowed to never make himself so vulnerable again. For the next several years, he turned to casual flings with no strings attached. It had worked for him until Laura came into his life.

Being with Laura made all those old feelings surface once more. Try as he might to resist, he was falling for her. It terrified him. People fell in love all the time. Other people. Not Cooper.

He spent too much time thinking of Laura. And there she was in his house. And he liked it. He liked having her there. Heck, Duke even liked her.

A gust of sea wind whistled, sending the falling snow swirling. How had one woman managed to turn his life upside down?

EIGHT

The next morning, Laura woke up to the rosy hue of dawn filtering through the guest bedroom window. Despite the unexpected events of the previous day, she'd slept surprisingly well. She stretched languidly, feeling refreshed and wonderfully energized for the first time in weeks. She snuggled deeper into the cozy warmth of the flannel sheets. *I should sleep here more often.* She stopped herself. *No. No, I shouldn't.* Choosing instead to dwell on more practical matters, she sat up and made some phone calls, showered and dressed, then headed downstairs.

The now-familiar open-concept living area welcomed her with its soaring ceilings and large windows. But the morning sun flooded the space with natural light. A breathtaking view unfolded before her eyes. The house sat perched on a hill overlooking the picturesque harbor of Mistletoe. The snow-dusted ice dotted with boats was a tranquil backdrop that added to the charm of the house.

She was searching for coffee when Cooper arrived, looking attractively sleepy. Looking that good in the morning really set the bar high. He asked her if she'd slept well.

"Fantastic! In fact, it's the best night's sleep I've had since I moved here."

He grunted. "I wish I could say the same."

"Oh. Sorry. Was I too loud this morning?"

Cooper raked his fingers through his hair. "No, not at all. It's me. I just couldn't sleep."

"If you tell me where it is, I'll make coffee."

The kitchen hadn't seemed small until the two of them started making coffee together. Cooper pulled some coffee out of the cupboard and filled the coffeemaker with water, while Laura ground the coffee and got out two mugs. At every turn, they seemed to be in each other's way, reaching in the same direction then apologizing and turning, only to bump into each other the next moment—all the while apologizing and saying "excuse me" until they had to laugh. As they stood face-to-face, inches apart, their laughter faded. Cooper's gaze wandered from her hair to her lips.

Her phone rattled on the countertop. Laura flinched and looked around. "That might be the tow truck. I called earlier." She glanced at her phone, but she would have to reach past Cooper to get it. He followed her gaze, picked up the phone, and handed it to her.

"Delia." She turned the phone face down and whispered, "My sister." After stepping from the counter, she settled on a stool on the kitchen island and continued the call. FaceTime would not have been Laura's choice, but it was too late. She should never have answered. She blamed it on her precaffeinated brain. The best she could do at that point would be to end the call with a promise to call Delia back.

"I figured by now you'd see how boring small-town life is and be ready to move back."

Laura inwardly groaned but assumed a cheery demeanor. "I love it here."

With a sigh, her sister said, "Well, I guess if you don't mind staring at water."

"Actually, I don't mind it at all. It's tranquil."

"As in boring? I agree. But what about dating? I mean, I guess it's okay if you like grizzled fishermen with yellow rain slickers and pipes."

"Which I do, funnily enough." Laura's eyes flitted toward Cooper, whose broad smile spread to his sparkling eyes as he quickly turned and busied himself pouring coffee. "Look, Delia, I'm going to have to call you later. I've got a tow truck on the way." She immediately wished she could take those words back.

"A tow truck! Don't tell me you've been in an accident! Are you okay?"

"I'm fine. The car is probably fine. I just hit some black ice on the way home last night."

Delia sighed. "Oh, thank God. So you made it home okay, obviously. By the way, I love your new house."

Laura froze. That early in the morning, if she explained that it wasn't her house, Delia would suspect she'd spent the night. She would never hear the end of it. "So, I've got to go so I'll be there when the tow truck arrives."

"Be where?"

"Oh, it's just a short walk away." Having dodged a tricky topic, Laura felt her panic subside.

"Well, the reason I called was to remind you of the party tomorrow. You're going to be there."

It wasn't a question. There was nothing Laura would like more than avoiding that party. It was a big event every year, at least in Delia's mind, so Laura wouldn't disappoint her. That said, she wouldn't enjoy it.

Delia chuckled. "I don't have to ask you if there'll be a plus-one."

That remark stung so much that it took her a moment to recover.

Cooper said, "I'm free tomorrow."

Delia's eyes practically doubled in size. "Who was that?"

Laura realized her mouth was hanging open. "Oh, that?" She glanced at Cooper and back. "That's just Cooper. He's doing some work on my house." It wasn't a lie. He just wasn't doing that work at the moment.

Cooper frowned when she called him *just* Cooper, so she offered an apologetic shrug.

Delia's surprise quickly turned to suspicion. "Don't be rude. Introduce us." She assumed her polite manners and smiled.

Laura froze, eyebrows together, mouth open, unable to think of what to do next.

Cooper walked over, stuck his head in the range of the phone camera, and gave her a winning smile. "You must be Delia."

It was almost worth all the discomfort to see her sister so discombobulated.

"Yes. And you're Cooper." Delia giggled. "Obviously."

Laura watched, astonished. Speechless was a great look for Delia. Laura wished she would try it more often.

Delia was thoroughly focused on Cooper. "I was just telling Laura she's welcome to bring a plus-one to the party tomorrow. So, if you're not busy, we'd love to have you." She smiled, having regained her well-practiced poise. But Laura detected a devious glint in her sister's eyes.

Cooper, as calm and controlled as Laura was not,

said, "I'd love to." With a quick glance at Laura, he said, "It was great meeting you, Delia, but we've got a tow truck to meet."

"Oh. Of course! See you tomorrow, I hope!" Cooper stepped away, and Delia's delighted tone of voice changed only slightly but enough for Laura to catch the implication that they would talk later. "Bye, Laura."

"Bye." After double-checking to make sure she'd ended the call, Laura turned to Cooper. "What just happened?"

His face was a mirror of her shock. "I'm sorry, Laura. I didn't like the way she was talking to you."

"Do you realize what you've done?" she exclaimed, her mind a whirlwind of thoughts.

"I'm sorry. I had no right to impose like that." His eyes clouded with guilt.

Laura shook her head, an incredulous laugh escaping her. "Don't apologize to me. It's you I'm worried about. You don't understand what you've just signed up for."

Cooper looked crestfallen. "Right. Okay. I get it."

Seeing his disappointment, Laura rushed to clarify. "Not that I wouldn't love to have you there. But these people, my sister's friends, can be cruel."

Cooper tilted his head, confusion creasing his brow. "In what way?"

"They just make you—well, me—feel like I'm not

good enough. Like I'm a loser," Laura admitted, her gaze falling to her hands.

"Loser?" Cooper repeated, the surprise in his voice almost comical.

She shrugged. "It's just... what they do. And you'd be guilty by association and therefore a target. I wouldn't do that to you."

Cooper's smile bolstered her. "I love a challenge. If you take me, we can face them together." The warmth in his eyes made it impossible to refuse him.

She had so many questions, such as: why was he offering to go with her? But her most pressing issue was trying to figure out what to make of his cheerful enthusiasm.

Cooper said, "So it's settled. Tomorrow. What's the dress code?"

With an incredulous shake of her head, she gave up. "It's semiformal. Suit, tie. It's not too late to change your mind."

He apparently found that amusing. "What time?"

"We should probably leave here by six."

"Six it is." Cooper flashed a grin and headed upstairs to work, leaving Laura alone with her whirl-wind of thoughts.

By NOON, the oil had been delivered, and the tow truck had pulled her car out of the ditch. Cooper insisted it be towed to Enzo for a once-over to make sure there had been no damage. By the time they returned from the garage, Laura's life was once again back to normal.

For the rest of her afternoon, Laura finished unpacking and hung the few pictures she had. She was assessing the blank spots for wall hangings and furniture she needed to buy when Cooper arrived at the foot of the stairs. "I don't want to get your hopes up, but it's looking like I could be finished a week from today, which leaves you—"

"A finished house in time for Christmas! Thank you!" She almost gave him a hug but caught herself. They'd only recently become comfortable talking with each other. A hug could ruin it all, so she turned to business matters. "Oh, and good news. The insurance adjuster said I should have a check by tomorrow."

With a knowing nod, Cooper said, "Those folks have it down to a science, so I doubt my work will go over whatever they cover."

"Don't worry. I'm good for whatever goes over the insurance settlement."

Cooper frowned. "I'm not worried about that."

Laura felt the need to assure him. "I just didn't want you to think... I mean, you've done so much for me already."

He shrugged it off. "Not really. Your homeowner's insurance is paying me for the work. Oh, and did I mention my fee for the party?"

Laura's jaw dropped.

"Laura, I'm kidding!"

She wrinkled her face. "You might change your mind after tomorrow."

He leveled her with a look so soft and deep that Laura's heart fluttered.

"I won't change my mind." Abruptly, he turned and headed for the door. "See you in the morning."

As he closed the door behind him, he called out, "Lock the door."

Relieved that her knees didn't buckle beneath her, she did as he suggested. She was safe in her house, but her heart was in danger of falling.

NINE

AFTER ALLOWING TOO much time to get ready for her sister's party, Laura was dressed early and pacing in front of the fireplace, waiting for Cooper to arrive. When she heard his truck pull into her driveway, she smoothed down her tea-length deep-red velvet dress and took a deep breath. She was ready. What she wasn't ready for was opening the door to the sight of Cooper in a dark suit and tie, completely transformed from the rugged handyman she knew into the elegant banker he once was. Although no one at her bank ever looked anything like that.

She smiled. "You clean up pretty well."

He responded with a crooked grin. "I could say the same, but it wouldn't do you justice. You look gorgeous."

She gave him a mischievous look. "What? This old thing?"

He laughed as he helped her with her coat then offered his arm. "Shall we?"

She took it long enough to step outside and realize she couldn't locate her door key one-handed. It was a shame that she had to slip her hand from his arm.

After Laura insisted on driving, they headed for her car, and she took the wheel. "I know the way like the back of my hand, as well as all the alternate routes."

Cooper leaned back in his seat, watching the landscape pass by in a blur. "So, tell me about your family."

"Well"—she smiled as she used her turn signal—"my dad is an accountant, and my mother's a nurse. You've already met my sister, at least over the phone. That's pretty much it."

Cooper nodded. "What about you? I know you're an accountant."

"Unfortunately, yes. I come from a long line of accountants, so there was never any question about my career. I don't hate it exactly, but I'd give it up in a heartbeat if something else came along."

"That sounds like how I felt about banking. I could do it, but I didn't love it."

"Do you love what you're doing now?"

He didn't hesitate to answer. "I do. The handyman work is really just a side hustle. It's satisfy-

ing. I enjoy doing a job and seeing it finished. It's grat-
ifying, and in the end, it helps people. There's a little
of that in my main source of income. I like taking a
house that might not be in the best shape and turning
it into something special. It adds a little more charm
to the town, and it enables me to live here. I might not
be changing the world, but I'm making a small piece
of my world a little better."

Laura sighed. "That sounds so nice. I envy you
for that. After the new year, I start a new job. I'll be
working from home, so that's an enormous improve-
ment. But it's still accounting. Maybe someday, I'll
find something fulfilling like you have."

He leaned back and stretched his long legs before
him. "You deserve to do something you love."

"Thanks. But everyone does, don't you think?"

He squinted, considering it. "Not everyone. Most,
maybe. But there are people out there who deserve so
much worse." He grinned.

Laura laughed. "Unfortunately, I'm afraid you'll
meet some of those people tonight."

THEY ARRIVED at Delia's townhome to find a
bustling party, the air thick with laughter and music.
Delia rushed over to greet them. After Cooper helped
Laura out of her coat, Delia led him to the spare room

that was serving as a cloakroom. Laura started to follow, but a familiar voice sang out her name, and she cringed. *Tessa Fitzgerald*. Laura supposed it was best to get the worst over with. And Tessa was that— intelligent, pretty, and caustic.

Laura turned to find Tessa in an emerald-green dress that clung to her slim figure except for the pushed-up cleavage that billowed from her plunging neckline. Her bright blue eyes sparkled with conde-scension as she smiled at Laura.

Laura donned her most pleasant expression. "Tessa. Hello."

Tessa cooed. "Oh, look at you in your red dress! How cute! You came dressed as Mrs. Claus! Did you bring a jolly fat man in a red suit?"

Cooper appeared at Laura's side. "No, she brought me."

Tessa's smile vanished as she caught sight of Cooper.

Laura couldn't fault her for that. It might have been the soft lighting, but Cooper seemed to get hotter each time she looked at him.

Tessa eyed Cooper with remarkable attention to detail then practically purred, "And who are you, one of Santa's helpers?"

Cooper's response was polite but unmistakably chilling. "No, I'm Laura's date."

Tessa's friends Courtney and Blair practically

tripped over each other to join the group and get Cooper's attention.

Blair twirled a strand of her long brunette hair. "Where did you say you're from, Curtis?"

"Cooper. I didn't."

Courtney shook her head, sending her straight corn-silk bob rippling back and forth. "Don't mind her. She doesn't get out much."

Blair turned her head sharply but held her tongue.

Courtney sidled closer, nearly edging Laura out of the way. "But seriously, how did you two meet?"

"We live in the same town."

Courtney peered at him with what Laura had to admit was an engaging smile. "That must be quite a town."

The same old feeling returned—the churning in the pit of her stomach and the dread of what might come next. Within minutes, Delia's friends had ruined the most magical part of her new life—knowing Cooper.

Courtney gazed into Cooper's eyes. "So, where is this town? It sounds like a fabulous day trip." Her face lit up. "I know! You could show me around."

Cooper's lips spread to a smile that didn't reach his eyes. "There's a map on the town's website." He turned to Blair and Tessa, whose mouths were agape. "It was nice meeting you ladies, but Laura promised me a tour of the buffet table. Laura?" He gestured for her to lead the way, touched her back, then slipped his hand down to hers and gave it a reassuring squeeze.

As they left the initial unpleasantness behind them, they happened upon Laura's parents, Bill and Pamela. As soon as the introductions were made, Laura's father commandeered the conversation.

"So, Cooper, how did you and Laura meet?"

Laura said, "The first time it rained—"

Bill interrupted. "I asked Cooper."

Other than a moment of narrowing his eyes, Cooper barely reacted. "Her roof leaked, and I fixed it."

Bill said, "That's handy—being able to fix things."

Cooper nodded confidently. "Especially in my line of work."

"And what's that?"

Cooper grinned. "I'm a handyman."

A sharp look from her father nearly put an end to the conversation, but Laura's mother rescued them all from the awkward silence, saying warmly, "I admire people who can work with their hands. I've tried my hand at gardening and needlework. I'm not very good at either. Laura, on the other hand, can grow anything. Come spring, she'll have her yard blooming with colorful plants."

From there, the conversation went to Christmas

shopping and the weather. Then Laura declared she was starving and led Cooper, by way of the buffet table, to a corner to hide. On the way, Cooper grabbed a couple of glasses of champagne. Once they'd settled behind a large umbrella plant, Laura turned to Cooper. "I am so sorry about the third degree from my father—not to mention my sister's friends. I never intended to put you through all this. And here you were just trying to be nice."

He shrugged as though it were nothing.

"You're so lucky to have normal friends."

"Who, Enzo?" He laughed. "You're right. I am lucky. We've been friends nearly all our lives, since before kindergarten. And we know everyone else— enough so that no one ever dares mess too much with anyone, because we've all got too much ammunition."

Laura took a sip of champagne. "I didn't have too many friends in school. Most of Delia's friends had younger siblings who picked up where their older brothers and sisters left off—torturing me. You've met them. You can only imagine... I was pretty bookish by nature, but having so-called friends like that made it worse." She glanced around at the assorted conversational groupings scattered about the room.

She leaned closer. "We could grab a couple of those shrimp cocktail forks and start digging. How long do you think it would take to tunnel our way out of here?"

Cooper shook his head and sighed. "If only you'd worn pants instead of that pretty red dress. We could have hidden bags of dirt in our pants like in *The Great Escape*."

Laura played along, nodding. "You know that dirt-in-the-pants bit had to be uncomfortable. The rope burns alone..." They burst out laughing, causing heads to turn, which blew their cover. "Maybe we should wander and pretend we're enjoying ourselves."

He gazed into her eyes with that honest, unwavering gaze of his and said, "I am enjoying myself."

If he kept looking at her like that, she could fall deeply in love. And he did. She looked down at her almost empty champagne glass and took a sip. It was all she could think of to do that didn't involve losing herself in his gaze and either confessing feelings she didn't know him well enough to have or falling into a faint. The odds were fifty-fifty for either.

Tessa's voice cut through the cocktail murmur. "Oh, look what you're standing under!"

If Laura hadn't looked up, she wouldn't have had to discover that someone had rigged up the cat's toy, and Courtney was dangling mistletoe from a fishing rod over their heads. Her gut instinct was to flee, but she looked.

In a full panic, Laura started to leave, but Cooper, apparently not one to shy away from a challenge, took Laura's hand and drew her closer. His lips, of which she was now acutely aware, spread into a gentle smile. Laura's heart raced as Cooper drew closer, his eyes trailing down to her lips. Time seemed to stand still as he gently cradled her face and tenderly kissed her on the forehead. Had he done that at any other time—preferably not under duress—she would have swooned, but under the circumstances, it was awkward. Her pounding heart didn't help matters.

Tessa folded her arms. "Foreheads don't count. It's got to be lips."

Laura whispered, "It's okay. You don't have to."

But with a look both defiant and tender, Cooper kissed her on the cheek then brushed his lips against hers before planting a soft kiss on her lips. The warmth of it spread through her body until she nearly forgot where she was and melted against him. A shiver ran through her as his mouth moved over hers. After a lingering moment, they parted, both left breathless and stunned. Laura's eyes fluttered open, and Cooper stared into them while Delia's friends stood speechless, their taunts silenced.

"Wow," Laura whispered, her cheeks flushed.

Cooper smiled, his eyes brimming with warmth as he leaned closer and said softly, "I've wanted to do that for a while now."

Laura's heart soared. Then something came over her. Maybe it was the look in his eyes that over-whelmed her reason and apprehension. Whatever the cause, she grasped Cooper's lapel and kissed him. It was no peck on the forehead or soft lips brushed together. She kissed him with abandon, and he kissed her back as though it might be their last. For that matter, it might be. Laura had no idea how Cooper felt about it, except that their kiss deepened, and he tightened his arms around her.

A man's cough sounded. Convinced it was her father, Laura put her palm on Cooper's chest and gently pushed him away. Where that superpower came from, she didn't know, but they parted.

Delia's friends gaped. Her parents and Delia stood halfway across the room, staring. It appeared the party had come to a halt.

Cooper was the first to recover, declaring in a stage voice, "And that, ladies and gentlemen, is why the mistletoe tradition has endured through the centuries." He grinned, took Laura's hand, and said, "I don't know about you, but I've worked up an appetite." And with that, grabbing some champagne on the way, they escaped through the kitchen and up the back staircase, climbing and laughing their way to the top.

Cooper asked, "Where are we going?"

"There's a great view of the city from one of the bedrooms." She stopped, no longer laughing. "And... I need a quiet break from all the people."

"Okay." Not only did he seem to understand, but he didn't seem to mind. If his kiss hadn't sent her heart soaring first, that would have.

As Laura and Cooper made their way down the upstairs hallway, the sounds of the party faded. Laura stopped in front of a closed door and turned the handle. As she swung the door open, she froze. There on the bed sat her sister's husband, Philip, with his arms wrapped around Delia's best friend, Blair, their lips locked in a passionate kiss.

Blair was the first to notice their presence and, with a gasp, broke away from Philip's embrace, covering her mouth in horror. Philip's head whipped around, his face draining of color when he saw Laura. An agonizing moment of silence hung in the air as the four of them stared at each other in shock.

Finally coming to her senses, Laura hastily pulled the door shut. She staggered back a few steps, bile rising in her throat. Her mind reeled as she tried to process the image suddenly seared into her brain— Delia's husband cheating with her best friend. How could she tell her sister?

Heart pounding, she headed for the stairs, nearly stumbling in her haste. Cooper stopped her on the landing. "Laura?"

"That was Delia's husband, Philip. It was probably hard for you to recognize him since he was too busy making out with my sister's friend Blair."

"Oh."

Feeling lost, she looked at Cooper as if he had an answer. "I should tell Delia. But I can't tell her tonight. This is her big party. She looks forward to it every year. What should I do?"

"I can't tell you that. All I can say is to trust your gut feeling."

"My gut tells me that this sort of news can wait."

With a sympathetic nod, Cooper said, "We could leave now, if you want."

Between kissing Cooper and finding her brother-in-law kissing someone who wasn't her sister, Laura's head was spinning. "No. Delia would know something was wrong. Let's give it an hour." So they lingered as if nothing was wrong, talking some more with Laura's parents and Delia's friends until it almost felt normal. When a few guests left, Laura took that as her cue, and they made their escape.

Cooper offered to drive, and Laura let him. Freshly fallen snow crunched under their tires as they pulled out of the driveway, and the pale moonlight lit their path. Once home, Laura paused at her door. Catching a whiff of the surrounding pine trees and the neighbors' fireplace smoke mixed with a faint hint of Cooper's cologne, she was completely undone. Before she lost all control, she turned to unlock the door.

"Laura."

With her hand placed on the doorknob, Laura turned to see the same confusion in his expression that she felt. Their mistletoe kiss had suddenly changed things between them. Other than Delia's dallying husband, which she tried to block out, Cooper's kiss had dominated her thoughts during the quiet ride home. She was hopelessly attracted to Cooper, and she had been since she'd met him. But like the accounting she did for a living, things were meant to occur in a predictable order. Relationships followed a logical progression.

In the olden days, couples had courtships to take all the guesswork away. They just had to go through the process. Not that she would want to live in those times with those rules, but there was a certain comfort in knowing the order of things. But the kiss at the party had been so out of order. Neither of them had expected it. Laura barely knew anything about the guy, and yet all she could think about was his lips against hers.

Whatever was happening between them had suddenly shifted into warp speed. If their relationship didn't go as hoped, it could upend the new life that she'd planned for herself. Yes, she was crazy about him, but early feelings like that could cloud a person's good judgment. If it was meant to be, it could wait.

But she couldn't.

As they stood at her door, the air between them was charged with electricity. Slowly, Cooper leaned in, hesitating just before their lips met. The anticipation was exquisite torture. Unable to wait any longer, Laura closed the distance between them. The kiss began tentatively at first, both savoring the newness of the moment. The kiss was real. No one was watching or forcing it on them. Soon passion ignited, and Laura threaded her fingers through Cooper's hair, pulling him closer. Lost in the heady rush, they clung together. Cooper's brawny arms encircled her waist.

When at last they broke apart, breathless and flushed, Laura knew in her heart that it was meant to be. No kiss had ever felt more right.

Amid the emotions coursing through her, a brisk wind from the sea swept ashore and chilled her through, reminding her that inside, it was warm. But going inside would lead her to a place she couldn't go. She wasn't ready for where her impulsive yearning would take her. Cooper would never hurt her on purpose, but succumbing to the moment would give him the power to break her heart. It was too soon to risk that. So, ignoring the wind and the cold, Laura melted into the warmth of his arms and savored the moment as he kissed her again.

When it ended, he slowly shook his head. "Laura Everly." He gazed with a look of wonder, and time seemed to stop. It was as if they were each deciding what to do next.

With an abrupt good night, Cooper kissed her on the cheek and headed to his truck.

Once inside her house, Laura leaned on the door for a moment, then, tired but not ready to sleep, she turned on the fire and sank into her chair with two vivid thoughts on her mind: Cooper's kiss and the sight of her sister's husband with Blair.

With a sad sigh, she whispered to herself, "I'll have to tell Delia tomorrow." She groaned. "I wish someone else would. Anyone but me."

TEN

COOPER ARRIVED EARLY with a pair of plumbers and had a tile guy scheduled for the afternoon, all in an effort to finish the work before Christmas.

Laura appreciated how hard they were working but wished for time alone with Cooper. The events of the party had changed things between them. She wanted to believe it was for the good, but he was all about work now. Could he be having second thoughts?

While Cooper worked upstairs, Laura busied herself hanging pictures, shelving books, and installing curtains, but her mind was on Cooper. His kiss at the party might have been no more than a gesture of kindness to spare her from Delia's friends, but once home, he didn't have to kiss her good night. That had to mean something.

Desperately, she wanted something—anything—

to break the silence between them, but it wasn't coming from her. Courage failed her. The longer she remained silent, the worse it would be. In a sudden bold move fueled by desperation, she walked toward him and stumbled over the words. "Cooper, w-why did you kiss me last night?"

He turned around slowly, his eyes wide open in apparent surprise. His mouth opened then closed again without uttering a single word.

Laura didn't know how to feel about Cooper's silence. She only knew it was unbearable, and she needed to break it.

"Please say something," Laura whispered, her voice barely above a breath.

Cooper closed the distance between them and quietly said, "Because I wanted to."

Unable to believe him, Laura said, "Because if it was to save me from Delia's friends, I just wanted to thank you. It was a kind thing to do."

Cooper shook his head. "I wasn't being kind. I couldn't stand seeing you hurt. I had to do something. I don't know..." He looked thoughtful but reserved. "Maybe I just wanted to shield you from them."

Laura glanced downward to hide her disappointment. It was far from the answer she'd hoped to hear. Still, despite his assurance to the contrary, it was a kind thing to do. "But you kissed me good night. You didn't have to do that."

Frowning, he shook his head. "That was a mistake."

His words felt like a stab in her heart.

His forehead crinkled in concern. "I've hurt you. I'm sorry. The truth is, they forced a situation we weren't ready for. And... I got carried away."

Maybe he wasn't ready for it. When she first caught sight of him in that suit, all dressed up for the party, he could have kissed her right there—for as long as he wanted. She felt as though she had tripped and fallen—for him. But now all she could feel was the pain from the fall. When she was able to, she lifted her eyes to meet his.

Cooper said gently, "We're just getting to know one another. Let's give it some time."

Laura nodded easily enough. "Sure." *Time.* She forced a smile. "That makes sense." And it did. But her heart didn't care about sense.

A worker called out from upstairs. Cooper glanced upward, gave her shoulder a squeeze, and headed up to work. When he was well out of sight, Laura grabbed her purse, scribbled a note saying she'd gone out to run errands, and left it taped to the door with a piece of packaging tape.

With no actual errands to run, Laura went to a dockside café, where she stayed for a couple of hours, drinking coffee and watching the waves. The serenity in the ocean's movements soothed her aching heart.

Cooper hadn't rejected her outright. And upon

reflection, she probably needed as much time as he did. Her move to Mistletoe was the culmination of a dream. She'd planned it for her favorite time of year, Christmas. She hadn't expected how emotional it would be. By the time the events of the party had unfolded, her emotions were raw. Cooper's kiss tipped her over the edge.

Christmas was an emotional time. Jumping into a relationship was an emotional step, and the holiday season added pressure. Perhaps taking time was a wise thing to do, or perhaps it was merely a way to let her down easily. She wished she knew which it was.

WHEN SHE COULDN'T PUT it off anymore, Laura headed home. As soon as she walked in the door, Cooper came halfway down the stairs. "Come on up. I've got something to show you," he said cheerfully.

At first, jarred by his remarkable ease, she realized he'd moved on as though nothing had happened. She had to adjust. Drawing in a deep breath, she followed him up to the bathroom. "Wow! It's completely transformed! It's so much better than before." She gasped. "Is that a heated towel rack?"

Cooper grinned. "And the floor's heated too."

Stunned by the unexpected upgrades, Laura said, "But we never talked about that!"

"I threw them in because I thought you'd enjoy

them," Cooper replied, his eyes shining with pride. He added, "At no extra charge."

Overwhelmed, she fought the impulse to throw her arms around him. The next moment, she wished he would stop being so nice. "I love it. It's perfect," she said, her voice filled with genuine wonder. "I don't know how to thank you."

"Join me for lunch?"

Laura hesitated, feeling as though she were on an emotional roller coaster. She struggled to reconcile the conflicting signals he was sending. Of course, lunch sounded great, but if they both needed time, that wouldn't help her throttle back her feelings. As for him, he was on his own because she was thoroughly confused.

She was still trying to figure things out when he looked down with a bashful expression that was way too attractive. "I'm an idiot."

"Is this the part where I'm supposed to disagree?"

He smiled. "No, it's a statement of fact." His eyebrows drew together, prompting Laura to wonder if he might be as confused as she was.

Laura shook her head. "We don't have to have lunch. Like you said, we both need some time."

"Yeah. Now I feel guilty."

At least he knew what he felt. Laura didn't know what she felt anymore.

He exhaled. "I've been told I'm not good at expressing my feelings."

"I thought you did pretty well."

Cooper shifted his weight and leaned on the doorway. "After you left, it occurred to me that I might have given you the wrong impression."

Completely confused, Laura said, "What's the right impression?"

"That... I've been burned, and it's taken me a while to recover. I'm still getting to know you."

Maybe it was her accounting brain kicking in, but it was like looking at numbers, and numbers didn't lie. There were credits and debits, and life didn't look as good from the debit side of the ledger. "Well, so far, it looks like I got the right impression."

"Except the part about how I like you. A lot."

She didn't know whether to be frustrated or to swoon. Swooning was gaining some ground.

"When I said we weren't ready, I wasn't trying to let you down easy. I was afraid I was getting ahead of myself."

Laura supposed that sounded better, but she still felt apprehensive.

As he gazed at her, a bashful smile lit his face. "One thing's for sure. We've got the kissing part down."

Laura felt a blush come to her cheeks.

Cooper said, "But it took things to a new level. I hardly know you, but here's my impression. You're not the sort to take anything lightly, including relationships. So whatever we're going to have, I want to do it right."

Me too. Right here. Laura tried to calm her pounding heart. That was hopeless. The best she could manage was to murmur, "Okay."

He looked relieved. "So, I thought we might start with lunch."

"I like lunch." Then she remembered. "I forgot. I just ate."

"Coffee and dessert, then?"

"Okay. I'll have some pie while I watch you eat lunch."

And with that, the spark that began with their kiss burst into flame, but she had the good sense to suppress it. Her heart wasn't on the same timeline as his, but she could cope with that far better than rejection.

With the tension somewhat eased between them, Laura practically floated down the porch steps on the way to his truck.

Laura opened the door just as Delia pulled into her driveway.

Cooper asked, "Were you expecting company?"

"That's Delia's car. She wouldn't come here unannounced unless something was wrong."

Cooper said, "I can guess what it is. I'll tell you what. I'll go get us some takeout, and you two can talk." With a wave toward Delia's car, he backed out of the driveway.

ELEVEN

DELIA GOT out of her car and walked inside without bothering to explain why she'd come. Her red-rimmed eyes told enough of the story. She turned to Laura. "Why didn't you tell me?"

Laura led her to an overstuffed chair by the fireplace. "Can I get you some coffee or something?"

Delia shook her head.

As Laura sat down, the sight of the snow globe on the mantel made her uneasy. She thought back on her wish that someone else would tell Delia about Philip's indiscretion, but she'd never expected that it would be Philip. From what Laura had observed, Philip wasn't exactly in touch with his feelings, and Delia seemed more like a mosquito buzz in his orbit. She tried to imagine Philip, overcome by guilt, pouring out a confession to Delia. She supposed it had happened on its own, but she narrowed her eyes at the snow globe and wondered.

Delia said, "He's never been like Cooper is with you."

Laura turned from the snow globe. "Meaning?"

Admiration filled Delia's voice. "Cooper is so attuned to you. Philip has never been like that, but I always knew—thought I knew—he was there for me."

Laura got stuck on the idea that Cooper was attuned to her but forced herself to move on. "I would have told you, but you were so happy. You live for that party, so I thought I'd let you enjoy it and call you today after you'd had a chance to rest."

Delia rested her head on the back of the chair. "He said Blair threw herself at him."

"She was all over Cooper earlier in the evening, so it's not hard to imagine her throwing herself at Philip."

"Yeah, but he didn't have to catch her." Bitterness darkened her expression.

Laura didn't know what to say. She was inclined to believe Philip, but that didn't absolve him of guilt. He did confess, so that worked in his favor. But none of it mattered if the snow globe's enchantment had brought it about.

Delia said, "He insists it was only a kiss, but what might have happened if you hadn't walked in?"

Philip had never struck Laura as the unfaithful type. But what did that even mean? He didn't have to be the type to give in to temptation. But even if it was only once, how would Delia ever be able to trust him again?

Delia stared at the fire for a long while then blurted out, "And Blair! Blair thinks she can just kiss my husband and then trot off to work the next day at her daddy's cosmetics company without a care in the world!"

Which she apparently could, but Laura didn't say it.

Delia gazed at the flames and pouted. "I hope she slips and falls into a big vat of *Eau de la Mort*."

Laura sprang up and went to the snow globe. "She didn't mean that! She meant *Eau de l'Amour*!"

Delia looked up. "Who are you talking to?"

Laura thought fast. *The, uh, theoretical spirit of Christmas?* She wanted to bury her face in her hands. There was no way to explain why she'd just spoken to an inanimate object. But the spirit of Christmas? What did that even mean in that context? But she'd already said it, so she moved on, looking Delia straight in the eye. "It was a rhetorical statement. I mean, who says Santa Claus is just for kids? Maybe he's got a Christmas miracle in store for you. Maybe he'll... come down your chimney and bring you... a happy ending." She had just gone from bad to worse.

Delia's shoulders slumped, and she pouted. "My chimney could use a happy ending."

Laura winced but said nothing.

The back door opened and closed, signaling Cooper's return, much to Laura's relief. Amid burgers at the kitchen table, they enjoyed pleasant conversation about anything but Philip, then Delia's phone chimed to signal a text message. To her credit, she ignored it until it chimed again then rang twice.

Laura set down her burger. "Well, now I'm curious."

Delia picked it up and glanced at it. "It's just Courtney." Something caught her eye. "Oh, wow."

Laura and Cooper looked at her, both curious.

Delia looked wide-eyed at Laura. "There's been an accident."

"Who? Mom? Dad?" She sprang out of her chair.

Delia grabbed Laura's arm and pulled her back down to her seat. "No, they're fine." Stunned, she looked up at Laura. "It's Blair. She slipped and fell at work."

Thinking out loud, Laura whispered, "Into a vat of perfume?"

Delia said, "No. She was spraying perfume samples into the air, then she took a few steps and slipped on the perfume residue on the floor. She broke her toe."

Cooper stared in disbelief. "What a freak accident."

Laura whispered to herself. "The snow globe."

Cooper raised his eyebrows. "I'm sorry?"

Stunned to realize she'd said it out loud, Laura

looked at him with saucer eyes. Drawing a blank, she saw no way out and just said it. "It's the snow globe."

Cooper stared.

Delia wrinkled her face.

"The snow globe!" She looked from Cooper to Delia. "Okay, fine. You'll think I've lost my mind, but ever since I brought that thing home, strange things have been happening. Delia, what did you say before Cooper got back?"

Delia furrowed her eyebrows. "Uh, I said Blair thinks she can just kiss my husband and then trot off to work."

"No, after that," Laura said. "You wished..."

"That she'd slip and fall into a vat of *Eau de la Mort.*" Delia frowned at her sister. "I didn't mean literally."

"I know that, but the snow globe didn't! Thank God I corrected your French!"

"And what's wrong with my French?"

"Oh, nothing—except *Eau de la Mort* means water of death."

Her sister's jaw dropped.

Laura nodded. "Blair's perfume is *Eau de l'Amour*, water of love."

Delia leaned back in her chair and rolled her eyes. "Oh, come on, Laura. There's Christmas magic, and then there's Christmas magic. You know which one this is?"

Laura stared, unamused.

"The crazy kind!"

Laura turned to Cooper, hoping for some support, but all she got was a perplexed look.

"You talk to the snow globe?"

"Well, no, not routinely. But I just saved Blair's life."

Delia grumbled, "Not that she deserved it."

Cooper shook his head slowly. "Think about what you're saying."

Laura winced. "Believe me, I have."

With a pained look, he said, "You're saying the snow globe is magic?"

Laura rubbed her forehead. "Yeah."

Delia leveled a sober look at her sister. "And what about Santa Claus? Is he real too?"

Laura scowled. "Very funny."

Delia raised her shoulders. "I'm just trying to sort out the Christmas magic."

Laura tried to overlook the tone of voice her sister usually used with young children. "I know you don't believe me. I also know that things have happened that I can't explain." She let out a loud gasp. "Cooper!"

He thought she had lost it. There was no other way to interpret the look on his face.

"Never mind." She tried to appear calm, but she'd almost blurted out that the snow globe had brought Cooper to her. That assumed that he was, in fact, with her. They hadn't acknowledged that yet. Whatever they were to each other, bringing the snow globe into the mix would only complicate things, so she deflected. "They could've been coincidences."

Cooper's questioning look troubled her because she didn't have any answers. Delia unwittingly saved the day when she got up and went to the snow globe. "I wish Philip and I could go back to the way things were when we were happy."

Although Laura suspected Delia was making fun of her, she was glad to have the focus on somebody else. Delia's phone rang. She glanced up and whispered, "It's Philip."

Laura couldn't look at Cooper, but she felt his eyes on her. Delia answered the phone as she headed upstairs for some privacy.

Cooper said, "Tell me more about this snow globe."

There wasn't much she was willing to tell him. "I bought it at Jessica's shop in the village." Laura shook her head and shrugged as if that were the end of the story.

Cooper said, "It's the season. The month leading up to Christmas throws our lives out of balance. Our routines are disrupted by shopping and parties. Add to that moving and the rain damage to your home, and a few coincidences seem extraordinary because everything ordinary feels out of sync."

"I suppose." But as much as she wanted to, Laura couldn't buy into Cooper's explanation.

Delia came downstairs. "I'm going home. Philip has agreed to go to couples' counseling, so we're going to try to work things out."

"Good." Laura hoped it was good. She didn't know whether it was the right move for Delia, but it wasn't Laura's call. Delia believed she and Philip could get past his unfaithfulness, so Laura would support her. She gave her sister a hug and told her she loved her.

Minutes later, Laura watched Delia drive away then went back inside and stood at the fireplace and stared at the snow globe. Was she imagining its enchantment?

Cooper finished loading his tools into his truck then came back inside to join her. "You've got your house back now. I'll work up the costs and get that to you tomorrow. If it goes over the insurance appraisal, we can work something out."

"Thanks, Cooper. You did so much. I don't know how to thank you."

Cooper's eyes filled with warmth. "You do owe me a lunch, but I'd settle for dinner."

"I'd like that."

TWELVE

COOPER TOOK Laura to a restaurant on a hill, where they sat at a candlelit table overlooking the sea. Fresh evergreens wrapped in Christmas lights and red velveteen bows garlanded along the chair rails and beams lent a festive aura to the room.

Over dinner, Cooper said, "I moved back home because city life wasn't for me. I missed the tight-knit community, the familiar faces, the friends you can count on, and the pace." He paused, looking thoughtful. "It's not so much the pace as it is the fact that people savor the process of living."

Laura smiled. "That's why I moved here. I'm still close enough to family, so I think I've found the best of both worlds."

"And you're able to work remotely. Mistletoe is too long a commute for most people. It's our saving grace. We appreciate the tourism income, but it's always a bit of a relief when the season ends—at least for me. Life gets back to normal."

Laura said, "You're lucky to have the sort of work that lasts all year round. These historic houses must be in constant need of repair."

Cooper nodded, looking slightly amused.

"What?"

He shrugged. "I didn't say anything."

"But you're thinking about something. What is it?"

"Laura, the handyman work isn't for me." Apparently sensing her confusion, he said, "I don't need the money."

"Oh." She wasn't sure how to interpret that. Even wealthy people she'd known behaved as though they needed—or wanted—more money. The only difference was that at some point, their goal shifted from survival to a challenge. It was a sort of game for some people. But Cooper didn't seem overly focused on material wealth. His home, tastefully understated in style and perched on a hill overlooking the harbor, spoke of his wealth, but the fact that he downplayed it spoke even more of his character.

Laura waited while the busser cleared her plate, then said, "There's something about a small town that makes the status symbols of life seem less important. I suppose it's because of the things I enjoy in my daily life here. I love looking out at the sea, the way it looks different each time, a warm smile from a store clerk, shops that reflect the personalities of the owners, and the way people come together in good times and bad. I love it all, and they all have one thing in common— they aren't laser-focused on their jobs or their money."

Cooper's eyes brightened with shared understanding. "Exactly. Life is about more than that. It's about the beauty around us and the people we share it with."

Laura chuckled. "Although it's easy to discount money while sitting here sipping wine in a nice restaurant."

Cooper dismissed what she said with a shake of his head. "The restaurant is nice, but we could be in a dockside shanty eating out of a paper-lined basket, and it wouldn't matter to me. It's the company I'm enjoying." His gaze deepened. Nothing moved except Laura's heart, which was pounding.

She realized her gazing had turned into staring but got lost in his eyes and in thoughts of the man she was getting to know. With some effort, she looked away, hoping he couldn't tell how hard she was falling for him.

Cooper paid the check. "Shall we?"

As they walked to his truck, Laura lifted her chin to the cold air, which felt good on her flushed face. Over dinner, she'd felt as though they'd discovered an unspoken understanding that they were heading somewhere together but there was no need to rush.

Yet her nerve endings were on heightened alert every time he drew near. His hand touching her back as they walked out the door or his fingertips touching her arm to help her into the truck sent her into a state of lightheaded euphoria.

On the quiet ride home, Laura looked at the inches between them and resisted the urge to close the space. She reminded herself of his desire to take a step back, but while he did that, she stole glances at him, admiring his rugged features and the way his strong and sure hands gripped the wheel.

The contentment they had shared over dinner seemed a world away as they approached Cooper's house. An unexpected figure, a woman with a chic, short haircut, leaned against a car parked in his driveway. Cooper's eyes narrowed as he parked the truck.

Despite her curiosity, Laura didn't want to be caught in the middle of the situation. "Why don't you drop me off? We can have that nightcap another time."

Concern etched his face as he considered the matter. "Yeah, maybe that's for the best." The weight of his words lingered between them.

Don't ask. Don't look desperate or jealous.

Apparently inferring her thoughts, Cooper said, "She's my ex." He hastened to clarify, "Girlfriend, not wife! She's probably home for the holidays, although why she's on my doorstep, I can't fathom."

Laura could guess, but there was enough awkwardness in the air without her adding to it.

"Excuse me." He got out of the truck, walked over to his ex-girlfriend, and they exchanged a few words. When she looked over at the vehicle, it was all Laura could do not to slide down in the seat out of sight. *Of course this would happen because everything seemed perfect. So right.* It didn't take long to go from so right to so wrong.

As Laura tried not to watch them, she sought ways to minimize the situation. Everyone had baggage. If the tables were turned and Alan showed up on her doorstep, Cooper might be going through the same thing for no reason.

Alan. It was over with Alan before they even broke up. During their last few months together, Alan had become increasingly absorbed in his work. Laura understood work pressure; she had her own to deal with. But in time, maintaining an orderly home and clinging more tightly to routines weren't enough to mask her unhappiness.

It took her years to recognize the pattern she'd fallen into. While few relationships were perfectly balanced, she was remarkably gifted at what she came to think of as the end of a seesaw relationship, in which whoever she was involved with would, with no warning, hop off the seesaw and leave her to crash into a worn patch of dirt as a dust cloud obscured her dismay.

Her first serious boyfriend in high school had cheated on her with a close friend. To avoid dealing with the betrayal, Laura dove into schoolwork and extracurriculars, keeping herself fiercely busy. For two years, she avoided relationships. They only caused pain she couldn't bear.

In college, finally ready to take a chance on a guy, she fell hard for Matt, who was excitingly angsty until he revealed himself to be emotionally volatile, lavishing her with over-the-top romantic gestures one day then scowling and sulking the next. The unpredictability kept Laura on edge, never knowing what to expect. She found refuge in tasks she could control, like color-coding her class notes with index tabs and highlighters and planning every hour of study time, down to five-minute breaks to relax.

A string of dates and near misses stretched out over the next several years until, alone again and buried in work, she resolved to change her life. And she had! And yet, there she was, on a date—if that was what it was—with a guy, and his ex had shown up.

Cooper climbed into the truck and backed out of the driveway without saying a word. Laura replayed the scene in her head in a half dozen different ways. *Couldn't he have just told her to leave?* If he had, then what would have followed—a romantic nightcap together while his mind was on whatever was going on with his ex-girlfriend? Laura had compiled quite a list of potential scenarios by the time they arrived at her house.

As they pulled into her driveway, Cooper started to get out of the truck to walk her to her door, but Laura stopped him. "That's okay. Don't get out. Thanks for dinner." Cooper's mouth hung open as she turned and got out of the truck. Cooper dutifully waited until she was safely inside before leaving. As if he could hear her, she waited until he was gone before she muttered sarcastically, "Great. An ex-girl-friend. I hope they'll be happy." She gasped and turned to the snow globe. "Not really!"

Laura, look at yourself! It's a round piece of glass! She wrinkled her face. *But so are crystal balls.* "Which are not magic, either! They only have as much power as you give them." Her shoulders slumped as she sighed. The problem was that since moving in, she could trace every significant thing that had happened back to that snow globe. She walked over, turned it upside down and back, then watched the snow fly and settle gently down. "What's your deal?" she mused aloud, only to dismiss her thoughts, reminding herself that she'd been obsessed with the snow globe long enough. It was time to put that to an end. She would test it, it would fail, and it would all be over.

She took the globe and peered at it intently. "Do you want to know what I wish? I wish Cooper would come back here and tell me the truth about how he feels about me. No more Christmas magic. Just the truth."

Nothing happened. With a satisfied nod, she sank into her favorite chair. *Enough.* It didn't matter whether the magic was real or imagined. She didn't want to live like that anymore.

With a snort, Laura abruptly awoke and sat upright in her chair. A glance at the clock told her she'd dozed off for about twenty minutes. Headlights from the driveway shone through the window. Cooper's truck. She'd heard it too many times in the past couple of weeks not to recognize the sound. Her eyes darted to the snow globe. "What did you do?"

Still feeling unsettled about how she'd left things with Cooper, she got up, took a deep breath, and went to the door. She stood waiting for him to knock, yet when he did, she flinched. After a few calming breaths, she opened the door.

"Can we talk?" he asked, his expression unreadable.

Laura nodded, gesturing for him to come in.

They sat on the sofa in silence for a few moments before Cooper spoke. "I'm sorry about earlier."

"No, I'm sorry. You have nothing to apologize for. I was... uncomfortable, but I was rude to leave you so abruptly."

Cooper sighed, running his hands through his hair. "It was an awkward situation."

Disagreeing might have helped, but she couldn't.

"It reminded me we're only beginning to know each other, and there might be unfinished business."

Cooper bristled. "Oh, it's finished!" He softened his tone. "But you're right. Maybe we rushed into this."

Laura's chest tightened. That was not what she meant, but she stopped short of protesting for fear of seeming overeager. Sensing he had more to say, she remained silent but dreaded what might come next.

"I care about you, Laura. A lot."

She didn't realize her jaw had dropped until he asked, "What is it?"

Without thinking of what she was saying, she said, "The snow globe."

His face went through a couple of confusion-induced contortions. "What?"

She hesitated, knowing how she would sound— the same way people had sounded for decades when they told people they'd had UFO sightings or abductions. Then the government rebranded them into UAPs, said they were real, and everyone seemed okay with it.

Laura took a deep breath and exhaled. "Okay. So, I'll just give you the facts." Her eyes flitted toward him, but she couldn't look him in the eye. "I was a little disconcerted after you dropped me off. I came inside, and I..." She paused, reconsidered, then blurted it out. "I said I wished you'd come back here and tell me how you really feel. And you knocked at the door." She braced for his response.

He didn't laugh or recoil in horror. Worse, he looked at her seriously. "So that's why I'm here? The snow globe made me do it."

She thought she detected a hint of sarcasm. "I'm just stating the facts. You can draw your own conclusion."

Cooper got up and started slowly pacing.

That can't be good.

What he said next confirmed it. "You're describing coincidences. Come on, Laura. You're a logical person. Follow the logic."

"I know. I get it. But at some point, you just have to admit there's something going on here, and it's not logical. It's..."

The look he gave her made her inwardly shudder. "Magic?" He exhaled and looked away. "I love Jessica. She's a charming town institution. She's one piece of the puzzle that makes Mistletoe so appealing at holiday time. But she didn't just sell you a snow globe. She sold you a fantasy."

Laura nodded. "That's what I thought, but then things—coincidences—started happening."

Cooper slowly shook his head. "You know, one of the things I loved about you the first time I met you was your quirky obsession with organization. All the boxes were neatly stacked and clearly labeled with color-coded stickers. Meanwhile, the sky was literally falling. It was adorable." His eyes sparkled with amusement.

Laura couldn't share his amusement. He called it adorable. A therapist had once called it obsessive-compulsive. A disorder. She stared down and mumbled, "That's not what this is."

"No, it's not. It's not adorable. Laura, you're a bright and fascinating woman. I admire the way you took charge of your life and redefined it on your terms."

That sounded so nice, but she knew there was more.

"But you're letting this snow globe rule your thoughts and affect your judgment."

Laura felt like a deflated lawn decoration, a help-less eyesore on the holiday horizon. She couldn't draw in a breath, let alone speak. The best she could offer was a feeble nod. *So, is this it? Is this the part where he breaks up with me?*

As the weight of uncertainty hung between them, something shifted within her, and she lashed out. "I'll bet your ex didn't have a snow globe." The sharp look Cooper gave her in response made her wish she hadn't said it. "I'm sorry. That was petty."

"Sandra's in town for the holidays."

"That's nice." Laura tried to smile, but it was too late. She knew better than to voice her knee-jerk response, but ex-girlfriends didn't show up on doorsteps late at night just to say hello.

Laura's defenses were down, and she'd let her true feelings out. Maybe that was the snow globe's idea of a joke: getting Cooper's true feelings at the expense of sharing her own.

After kindly overlooking Laura's catty remark about Sandra, Cooper went on. "There's nothing between us anymore—at least not on my side. She knows that now."

Laura listened intently, a mix of emotions swirling inside her.

"That's not a problem for us."

Us who? You and me? You and Sandra?

"It's the kiss," he continued.

Confusion clouded her mind. "She kissed you?" *How did I miss that?*

"No!" He searched her eyes. "Our kiss—yours and mine." He ran his fingers through his hair. "This is not going well." He paused then spoke cautiously. "At the party... and after. At first, I was afraid I'd offended you."

"Offended me? No!" Laura felt a blush coming on. "It was nice. Not the kiss. That was better than nice. What I mean is they were trying to embarrass me, and you called their bluff. Anyone who can shut them up is a hero in my book." She grinned.

Relief washed over Cooper's face. "I'm glad to hear that."

Laura's eyes softened. "I blame my sister's friends for making you feel you had to do it out of pity."

Cooper's eyes widened in disbelief. "Pity? Is that what you think?" He shook his head in disbelief. "Laura, I like you!" A smile teased the corner of his mouth. "I'd like to think we might have gotten to a first kiss eventually. This just moved things up a bit."

Laura's heart skipped a beat. Unless she'd misheard, he'd just said that he liked her. "For the record, I like you too. So we like each other. Problem solved." She realized she was babbling nervously.

Cooper looked troubled. "It was never a problem. For me, anyway. I wanted to kiss you the moment I saw you in that red dress, looking so pretty. I mean, you look pretty in jeans and T-shirts, whatever you're wearing, because you're you."

As much as she loved hearing those words, Laura felt embarrassed by the whole situation. Yes, her sister's friends were horrible humans, but she suspected an even worse culprit. "This is my fault."

A soft smile lit his eyes. "You can't help being you."

Her heart raced with apprehension, but the truth spilled out. "Cooper," she confessed, her voice filled with vulnerability, "none of this would've happened if it weren't for the snow globe. It's making us feel things we wouldn't otherwise feel."

He lifted his palms. "Okay, hold on. This snow globe is a harmless Christmas decoration. Whatever we feel is between us."

"I know, but things have been happening. They didn't used to happen like this."

"And by *things*, you mean coincidences. We've talked about that."

He clearly did not understand, so she had to drive home her point. "Okay. I don't like admitting this, but when you dropped me off, I was a little jealous."

"It's understandable, and I'm sorry. I've explained how things are."

Laura nodded. "Exactly. Because I wished you'd come back and tell me the truth. And here you are."

Cooper heaved a sigh. "It's not the snow globe. Our timeline is off. The events of the party…"

The kiss?

"Pushed things up. It feels way too early to be discussing our feelings."

"But are they your feelings?"

"I'm the only one here." He frowned, looking thoroughly confused.

Laura was really beginning to wish she hadn't gone down that road, but it was too late. "Come here." She got the snow globe and showed him the figurine in front of the tiny cottage. "When I first got this, I looked at that guy there. I guess I was in a good mood, maybe feeling a bit silly." She hesitated. "I wished Santa would drop a hot guy like that down my chimney. And then you showed up."

With a confused chuckle, Cooper said, "Thanks…

I guess. But that didn't really happen. I'm pretty sure I came through the front door."

"Close enough! The next thing I know, my roof's leaking, and you walk in like a knight in shining armor—"

"I don't have any armor, but I was brandishing a nail gun and a tarp."

"Close enough."

Cooper looked off into the distance as if deep in thought. "Okay. Here's what I think. Christmas is an emotional time. On top of that, you've had a major life change since moving here. And I don't know what you've gone through in the past, but by the time we reach thirty, everyone's got some history and probably baggage. So it's understandable if—"

"No, it isn't. Granted, it's weird. But I wished you into my life, so whatever you feel might not be real."

Cooper said gently, "What I feel is that you're sounding a little nutty."

"Oh, I know! I completely agree!" She collapsed on the sofa and stared at the ceiling.

Cooper sat beside her. "Laura, look at me." He touched her chin, and she lifted her eyes.

"It's okay. I don't blame you."

"For what? Oh, for losing my mind."

Looking barely patient, he said slowly, "No."

Laura nodded, insisting. "Oh yes. You think I'm a partridge short of a pear tree? A soprano short of a caroling quartet? A reindeer short of Santa's sleigh team? A—"

"Got it. But that's not what I think!"

"What do you think?" she asked, knowing the snow globe would make him tell the truth because she'd asked it to.

"I think you should take that thing back to the store where you got it."

She hadn't expected that. "Really?"

THIRTEEN

Laura sat gazing thoughtfully into the fire, absently turning the snow globe over in her hands. She watched the miniature snowflakes twirl while she considered all that had transpired since that fateful day she'd bought the mysterious object.

Cooper believed they were coincidences. If she were in his place, she might think the same thing. *City girl moves to a small town with dreams of an impossibly perfect Christmas. When a home mishap disrupts her plans, she fixates on a cherished depiction of her shattered holiday dream.* It made sense, except that didn't happen.

With a deep breath, she placed the snow globe on the mantel. Its true nature no longer mattered. Whether it was ordinary or extraordinary, she was taking it back. The only magic she needed was her connection with Cooper.

She held the globe close. "Cooper was right. You need to go back to the store. It's time to find a new home."

Laura sighed. *And for me to stop talking to you.* In an effort to dispel her last bit of doubt, Laura said, "Anything that's happened has done so by chance, and to prove it, I'll make one last wish. Bring me coffee and doughnuts—plain glazed, please."

In silence, the swirling snow slowly settled as if indifferent to her challenge.

Laura threw up her hands. "Well, there you have it. I have officially lost my mind." She was on her way to the kitchen for more coffee when a knock rattled her front door. Her heart thumped as she walked over and opened it.

"Cooper!"

Although she hadn't been expecting him, the real surprise was the cardboard carrier of two coffees in one hand and the box of doughnuts in the other. "You haven't had breakfast yet, have you?"

"No, but—"

"Good. I had a sudden craving for doughnuts from the bakery in town, and I hate to eat sugary baked goods alone."

Coffee and doughnuts?

Cooper's eyebrows went together. "Is this a bad time?"

Realizing she was frowning, Laura brightened her expression and stepped aside, inviting him in.

"No. Not at all. In fact, your timing is perfect." *Just perfect.*

On his way to the kitchen, he asked, "Plain glazed okay?"

Laura said softly, "Yeah. That's exactly what I asked for."

He tilted his head and peered at her. "Excuse me?"

Laura blinked, glancing between Cooper and the snow globe sitting innocently on her mantel. Still reluctant to believe it, she struggled to get out the words. "I just asked the snow globe to bring me coffee and plain glazed doughnuts, and then you showed up."

Cooper narrowed his eyes and looked into the distance. "Yeah, but how many times have I brought coffee and doughnuts while I worked on your house?"

"But you've finished the house."

"Yes, but now I'm working on you." His eyes sparkled. "Have I charmed you into finding me irresistible yet?"

Laura knew he was trying to lighten the mood, but she couldn't let it go. "Yes, but for all the wrong reasons." Her stomach knotted at the thought that Cooper's affection might not be real, simply a product of the globe's enchantment. *No. I refuse to accept that. What I feel for Cooper is real.* She was sure it was real on her part, but she couldn't vouch for Cooper.

Cooper grinned. "All I heard was yes." He sat

down and opened the doughnut box. "I think the main issue here is that you, lovely lady, are suffering from acute sugar deprivation."

Laura attempted a smile.

"Fortunately, I have brought you the cure. Come on. Eat your doughnut." He lifted one from the box and set it on a napkin beside Laura's coffee.

Cooper finished his doughnut and leaned back. "Do you know what you need?"

"Another doughnut?" Laura tried to play along, but it wasn't easy. The snow globe had really outdone itself that time. Suddenly aware that Cooper was eyeing her strangely, she picked up a doughnut.

Cooper leaned forward. "You've spent too much time inside. What you need is some fresh air and a healthy dose of our signature Mistletoe Christmas."

He might have a point. After all, that's why I moved here. She forced a pleasant expression. "It must be the paint fumes getting to me. Are you sure that the stuff you used didn't have lead in it?"

"Pretty sure. I mean, they haven't sold lead paint in decades. Although there might be some old stuff on your walls. You haven't been nibbling on the baseboards, have you?"

"Not lately." She grinned.

"That's good." Cooper took a bite of his second doughnut. "So, about today. Are you busy?"

"No. My day opened up once I canceled my paint-chip-eating binge fest."

"That's what I was hoping, because it's not the Christmas season until you've been to the Mistletoe Christmas Market."

Feeling guilty, Laura confessed, "Actually, I have gone a couple of times."

Cooper dismissed what she'd said with a smirk. "Not with me."

In the face of her worries, Cooper had coaxed a genuine smile from her. She couldn't think of anything she would rather do than spend the day with Cooper. Still troubled by the snow globe, she forced herself to set the issue aside. "Okay."

THE MARKET WAS EVEN MORE charming than Laura remembered. Fairy lights twinkled from every tree, building, and kiosk. Wreaths and garlands were draped from lamp pole to lamp pole, and the air was rich with the scent of pine, cinnamon, and roasted chestnuts.

Cooper tucked Laura's hand into the crook of his arm as they wandered from stall to stall, examining the handcrafted decorations and treats. His smile never faded, his blue eyes warming with pleasure each time Laura showed an interest in something.

"Hungry?" He nodded to a food stall with hot apple cider and gingerbread cookies.

Laura shook her head. "I'm pretty sure I hit my

sugar quota an hour ago, but knock yourself out."
Cooper's enthusiasm was contagious. She looked on
with delight as Cooper steered her to the stall.

"We'll have one of everything." As the clerk pack-
aged up their treats, Cooper assured her, "We can
work it off with a sleigh ride later."

"A sleigh ride? Yeah, that's a great cardio work-
out." Laura turned to him with a skeptical grin.

"I mean... we could walk, but where's the fun in
that?" He shrugged, but his eyes gleamed. "Look! It's
snowing. Come on. Let's go dashing through the
snow."

Laura threw her hands in the air. "Well, why
not?"

If the snow globe made that happen, she didn't
want to know. She was happy. Even if it didn't last,
she wanted to savor the feeling of being with Cooper.
It might be the closest she would ever get to falling in
love.

AFTER DROPPING off Laura to gift wrap her
Christmas market finds, Cooper swung by his mother's house with some baked treats from the market.
Having caught up on news from town, Maggie asked
about Laura. Before long, he was pacing in front of
the fireplace while his mother watched from her
armchair, a knowing look on her face. He ran a hand

through his hair, his mind racing. "I barely know her, really. But it's different. She's different."

"You care for her," his mother said gently. "That much is obvious."

"I do, but it isn't enough."

Maggie said, "She doesn't strike me as the needy or demanding type."

"No, she isn't. But she's got this strange snow globe obsession. Jessica, you know, from the antiques shop? She told Laura the snow globe was enchanted."

Maggie nodded. "Jessica's always been a little... ethereal where Christmas is concerned."

"That's one way to put it. That's fine. I'm sure it's great for business—telling cute little tales to go with each item in her inventory. But Laura has really taken that snow globe legend to heart. Which is weird, you know? I mean, Laura is an accountant. She comes from a double-entry world where everything has to balance."

"Except this."

He nodded. "Except this."

Maggie set down her knitting needles. "Maybe that's why she's taken it to heart. If the snow globe embodies everything she loves about living here, then what's wrong with a little Christmas enchantment? She's living the storybook life she dreamed of and worked hard to make happen. Maybe after she settles in, she won't need the snow globe anymore."

Cooper gave it some thought but shook his head.

"No. Sorry, but I just can't buy it. I like Christmas as well as the next guy, but the Christmas magic thing is just sounding a little... wacky."

Maggie smiled at her son. "You didn't used to find it wacky when Santa brought your gifts."

Cooper leveled a knowing look at his mother. "Because I was a child."

"But we all have a little of the child in us, don't you think?"

"No, Mom, that's just you." A smile bloomed on his face.

Maggie tilted her head. "Maybe so, but I feel sorry for people who have lost touch with their inner child—especially at Christmas. They don't know what they're missing."

"Unfortunately, that's not Laura's problem." He plopped down on the sofa and leaned his head back.

"It's like you're describing a different person from the woman I met. Laura seems so down to earth."

"She's more than that. She's perfect. I mean, I know she's not perfect. No one is. But she's perfect for me. With one large exception."

Maggie leaned back. "I think once the holiday season is over, things will calm down. She'll put the Christmas decorations away—including the snow globe—and things will go back to normal."

Cooper wanted to agree. "That makes sense, but... I hate to even tell you this because it sounds so unhinged."

Maggie's eyebrows went together. He had her complete attention.

"She thinks a few coincidences happened because the snow globe made them happen, including me. She is convinced that the snow globe brought us together, so what I feel isn't really what I feel. The snow globe made me feel it."

"Oh." She wrinkled her face as she tried to reason that out.

Cooper looked at her knowingly. "See what I mean? Even if I could overlook it, which I'm not sure I can, she'll never trust how I feel."

Maggie's eyes softened. "And how do you feel?"

Cooper shook his head and debated whether to say it out loud. "I know how I could feel if I let myself. I could... fall in love with her."

"That's the human heart for you. It's got its own kind of magic, and it rules the way we live our lives."

"I'd like to think I have a say in the matter."

"We'd all like to think that." Her eyes twinkled.

Cooper nodded, conceding the point. "But the heart is a miraculous organ that keeps us alive. It's a real force. A snow globe isn't. It can't make me feel anything I don't want to feel."

"Oh, I know that well enough! God knows for all of your life, I've tried to make you do things you didn't want to do without any success. So, if a little snow globe can do that, that's some Christmas magic!" She had a good laugh then sighed. "Have faith. The only real Christmas magic I know comes from God. So stay in close touch with him, and it'll all work out."

Cooper exhaled and stood up to leave. She was right. He didn't go to church very often, but he'd never stopped believing. Which might be why the snow globe business bothered him so much. He couldn't have a relationship with someone who let that come between them.

As they walked to the door, Maggie said, "Give it time. If Laura's the one for you, she'll come around and realize that the true Christmas magic is love."

Cooper gazed warmly at his mother, who'd always been there for him with her quiet wisdom. He gave her a hug. "Thanks, Mom."

She smiled. "Anytime."

THE NEXT MORNING, Laura stared at the snow globe, anxiety twisting her stomach into knots. She'd lost sleep over it, but she'd made a decision.

She picked up the phone and called Cooper. "Can you come over? We need to talk."

"Sure." His tone was gentle, which she hoped was a good sign.

Cooper arrived, looking apprehensive. Laura led him to the sofa, where they sat facing the snow globe. She got straight to it. "I don't want our relationship to be based on a snow globe. Whether it's magic or my imagination, it's coming between us." She couldn't meet his eyes. "And I don't know how you feel. I mean, I guess what I'm saying is that I'd like to find out what we could be to each other without the snow globe."

He looked relieved, but that almost made it worse.

She continued, "Which is scary because if it is the snow globe, then I'll lose you. Not that I have you. But... I'd like us to be something." She winced, hoping she'd made some sense.

Cooper took her hand in his. "It's okay. Whatever we are to each other, whatever we feel, is from us, not some Christmas decoration."

"Do you really believe that?" She lifted her eyes to meet his.

Cooper nodded. "I really do."

"Okay. Then I guess it's time to take it back to the store."

"Would you like me to go with you?"

Laura nodded. "I'll go get the box it came in."

FOURTEEN

Snow swirled around Laura and Cooper as they hurried down the snow-dusted sidewalk, the Christmas lights overhead casting a warm glow on the quaint village shops. Laura clutched the snow globe box tightly in her gloved hands. The once-enchanting little globe now felt like an unwelcome burden.

"What if Jessica won't take it back?" Laura asked, her breath fogging up in the chilly air.

"Let's hope she does," Cooper replied, shivering slightly.

"I mean, she did warn me it was enchanted, but I thought that was just part of her sales pitch."

"If she doesn't take it back, we'll just have to dispose of it some other way."

Feeling defeated, she smirked. "How? A silver bullet?"

"Don't be silly. We'll put a stake through its heart." His mouth twitched at the corner.

Laura wanted to share his amusement, but she couldn't. "But if something happens to it, we don't know what will happen to us."

Cooper cast a pointed look her way. "You're just making my point. We need that thing out of our lives."

Laura understood what he was saying, but he hadn't really addressed her concern. But they'd arrived in front of the store, so she set those thoughts aside. The window display twinkled invitingly, yet all Laura could feel was the uneasiness gripping her stomach. She glanced at Cooper, who offered a reassuring smile.

"Ready?" he asked, his hand on the door.

"Ready," Laura confirmed, returning his smile.

The bell jingled softly as they entered, and Jessica looked up from behind the counter, her silver hair catching the light. She arched an eyebrow, clearly not surprised to see them.

"Laura, Cooper," Jessica greeted them, her voice cool yet somehow welcoming. "Nice to see you! What's this?" She fixed her eyes on the package.

Laura felt relieved to set the box on the counter and have it out of her hands. "This snow globe is... too much."

Jessica's brow furrowed. "Too much? How so?"

"It's making things happen."

"Things?" Jessica's deep-blue eyes flickered with curiosity.

Laura nodded. "Things I didn't ask for. And not just me. My sister was a little upset and said something she didn't mean, and the snow globe made her wish come true. At least it didn't do permanent damage, but there were broken bones. Well, one bone. Her big toe."

Jessica's face seemed to be stuck in a curious squint.

"But think of the possibilities. It's scary." The more Laura tried to explain, the less sense she seemed to make.

Cooper said, "It's disrupting her life and mine in the process."

Laura said gently, "We were hoping you'd take it back."

Jessica said, "I don't understand."

Laura was desperate. "Please."

Laura and Cooper exchanged looks, then Cooper said, "Look, I don't believe in this stuff. To be honest, it sounds a little out there. But I can't deny stuff has happened. Laura's sure it's the snow globe."

Jessica shook her head as if confused.

Returning the snow globe was harder than Laura had thought it would be. "It kind of grants wishes, except they're not really wishes." When Jessica didn't seem to register any understanding, Laura continued. "Do you ever talk to yourself? No, you probably don't, but I do. It sounds crazy. But sometimes, I just voice my thoughts out loud without thinking. But since I got the snow globe, random things that I say seem to come true but not in ways you'd expect."

"Such as...?"

Laura winced. There was no way around it; she needed to give at least one example, no matter how nutty she sounded. "Well, when I first brought it home, I set it on the mantel and noticed there was a guy outside the little house—which looks surprisingly like my little house, I might add. Anyway, I was just being silly. I said something about how I wished Santa would drop a hot guy like that down my chimney."

She winced again and looked at Jessica. "I mean, people say things like that, don't they?" She shrugged.

Jessica seemed like she might be considering it, although maybe she was just being polite.

Laura started to steal a glance at Cooper, but she couldn't bear the thought of what she might see, so she focused on Jessica. "So, you'd think if it were just, you know, a typical magical... snow globe..." *Now you're sounding completely unhinged.* "It would just drop a guy down my chimney. That would be the literal interpretation, right?"

Apparently, seeing that Laura was struggling,

Cooper came to the rescue with his version. "Then Laura's roof started leaking, and she called me to fix it."

For the first time, Jessica looked as though she understood, and she turned to Laura. "That must be when you stopped in the shop, asking for a handyman."

Laura felt oddly relieved. Something she'd said had made sense. "Yes! Exactly! So then Cooper arrived on my doorstep to fix my roof and the damage the leak caused."

Jessica seemed to be waiting for something. Laura looked at Cooper as though he had the answer. Following Laura's lead, Jessica turned to him too.

Cooper's mouth opened, but nothing came out until he rolled his eyes and said, "She thinks I'm the guy she asked to be dropped down the chimney."

"The *hot* guy?" Jessica corrected with twinkling eyes.

Cooper narrowed his eyes at her then moved on. "Since then, there have been a series of coincidences that may or may not be related to the snow globe. Either way, it's causing some friction between us."

Thoroughly embarrassed, Laura was beginning to wonder whether she should've just kept the darn thing, then Cooper said something she hadn't expected.

Jessica raised an eyebrow. "Friction?"

Without flinching, Cooper said, "Yes, Jessica, friction. I like Laura, and I think she likes me. But neither of us will be able to discover our true feelings unless we get rid of that snow globe. Then we'll know for certain that our feelings are real and not some snow globe love potion." He winced, glanced at Laura, and looked straight at Jessica. "We can't go on like this."

Laura's heart stopped for a moment. She hadn't realized how close they were to... not being close. Cooper's version of events sounded absurd. Worse yet, he was clearly over the snow globe and nearly over her.

Meanwhile, something in Jessica's eyes made her appear on the verge of a smile. "Okay."

"Okay? That's it?" asked Laura.

"Of course," Jessica said nonchalantly. "However, I must caution you. These snow globes have a way of—"

That got Cooper's attention. "These? There are others?"

Jessica tilted her head matter-of-factly. "Oh. Didn't I tell you?"

Laura almost shouted but restrained herself and let out a more modulated, "No! I think I would've remembered something like that!"

Jessica said, "Oh. Well, there's a lovely man who makes these. He lives in the backwoods of Maine and makes one every year in his workshop."

With a snarky look, Cooper said, "His name

wouldn't be Santa, would it?"

Jessica smiled patiently. "No, it's Steve."

Laura gave him a sideways nudge with her boot. If he didn't lose the attitude, Jessica might change her mind.

Jessica said, "He's a bit of a recluse. He comes in once a year, just before Thanksgiving, and drops off a snow globe to sell on consignment. I wouldn't worry about the return. I don't think he does it for the money. I mean, what did you pay, ninety dollars? One of those per year isn't nearly enough to live on, is it?"

Laura felt guilty. "Look, I don't need the money. If you would just take it back and maybe sell it to somebody else, everybody wins."

"Well, that would spare me the awkwardness of explaining to Steve. He's such a dear man. I'd hate to hurt his feelings."

The whole situation was making Laura increasingly uncomfortable. "You mean he's never had one returned before?" She found that hard to believe.

Jessica shook her head slowly. "Nope. Never."

As if sensing that Laura was weakening, Cooper said, "Well, there's always a first time, and this has to be it."

Jessica picked up the snow globe. "I'll just put this back on the shelf." She passed halfway by and turned back to Laura. "I should warn you..."

Laura's stomach sank. *No, please. Not another warning.*

"Steve mentioned once that the snow globes had a way of finding their way to the person who needs them."

Laura nervously glanced at Cooper, wondering what Jessica's cryptic words meant. *What's it going to do, hitchhike back to my house?* She bit her lip and accepted the warning. "Oh. Well, I don't need it, so... problem solved."

Cooper ran his fingers through his hair. "Maybe it was a mistake and Laura wasn't the person it was meant for. So we're doing our part to get it back to where it belongs."

Jessica didn't look like she was buying Cooper's interpretation, but she returned the snow globe to its shelf.

Once it was safely in its place, Cooper said, "Thank you, Jessica."

"Yes, thank you," echoed Laura.

After wishing Jessica a merry Christmas, Laura and Cooper left the store. Outside, Laura shivered from more than the cold winter air.

Cooper said, "Well, that's done."

Laura sighed with relief. "Yeah, it is." *I hope.*

Cooper pulled Laura into his arms and gave her a reassuring hug and a kiss on the cheek. He paused, his eyes fixed on hers. "What are you doing the day after tomorrow?"

"That's Christmas Eve."

"I know. But that doesn't answer my question."

He'd caught her by surprise. "I don't really have plans. I used to go over to my parents' house on Christmas Eve, but since I've moved, I don't think they'd expect me to drive back and forth two days in a row, so... I don't know. I guess I'll be here."

"What about spending Christmas Eve at my house? Nothing fancy, but I promise I'll feed you. There might be a fire and possibly movies. What do you think?"

"Oh." What did she think? In the back of her mind, she'd had the idea that he might lose interest in her once the snow globe was gone. But his invitation had planted a seed of hope. "I guess I assumed you'd spend Christmas Eve with your mother."

"It's a fair assumption, but she volunteers Christmas Eve delivering toys from a toy drive, so we always get together on Christmas Day. So if you haven't got plans..."

Laura's heart filled with warmth. "Yes—I mean, no. I haven't got plans."

"Good. Then it's a date."

A date. "Good."

They stood smiling at one another until it became awkward. Cooper broke the silence with a grin. "Okay, then. Christmas Eve. See you later."

"Bye." Laura turned and started walking, barely able to remember where she was going. She was overreacting, yet she didn't care. She was thrilled at the thought of spending Christmas Eve with Cooper. Then she remembered she hadn't even asked what she could bring. And on Christmas Eve, she couldn't show up without a gift. She still had some last-minute Christmas shopping to do, so she added one more item to the list and headed for her favorite shops.

FIFTEEN

THE SCENT of fresh-brewed coffee and cinnamon filled the air as Cooper pushed open the door to the coffee shop. He spotted Enzo by the window and slid into the seat across from him.

Enzo spent the first fifteen minutes filling Cooper in on his life. Despite the endless flurry of child-centered activity that drove his friend to apparent exhaustion, Cooper envied him. Enzo might complain of fatigue, but to Cooper, it seemed like a very full life.

"Hey, don't forget you're babysitting next Friday."

Cooper grinned. "It's hard to forget since you remind me every time I see you."

Enzo's eyes darkened. "Look at me. This is the face of a desperate man. The wife and I need a night out, or we'll both go insane." His face brightened. "Not that they aren't three little angels."

Cooper chuckled. "Relax. I promise I won't bail on you."

Enzo exhaled. "Thank God." He grinned, took a drink of his coffee, and set the cup down with a clink. "So. You and Laura..." Enzo suppressed a smile as he leaned on his elbows.

Cooper stared, too stunned to speak for a moment. When he did, he made no effort to hide his sarcasm. "I'm fine, Enzo. Good to see you too."

Enzo's eyes lit up with amusement. "Roof trouble, car trouble. What else could come next except love?"

"I've known her for ten minutes."

Enzo leaned forward. "That's how you know it's real."

Cooper frowned. "No, that's how I know that it's too soon to tell."

Enzo shook his head. "Oh, come on, man. I've known you forever, which means, ten minutes or not, you like her."

Cooper shrugged and flagged down a server so he could order his coffee. "*Like* is a fair assessment of the situation."

"You ought to try lines like that on your girlfriend."

"She's not—never mind." He had fallen right into Enzo's trap.

Enzo leaned back, looking satisfied as he folded his arms. "Seriously, I'm glad you found someone."

Cooper had to correct him. "*May* have found someone. There are... issues."

Enzo nodded knowingly. "What, snoring? Flatulence?"

"No!" Cooper glanced around uneasily. "What made me think I could even talk to you about this?"

Enzo lifted his shoulders. "I don't know. Maybe thirty years of friendship?"

"Maybe. But so far, you're making it worse."

Enzo smiled warmly. "Sorry. You'd think I'd be better at old-married-guy advice by now. But I'm still as clueless as ever. Ask my wife."

"I wouldn't think of burdening her with my problems. She's got enough grief in her life with you."

"Yeah, lucky lady." They shared a laugh, then Enzo grew serious. "So, what's going on?"

Cooper sighed as he ran a hand through his hair. "It's this snow globe."

"Snow globe?"

"Yeah. She bought it when she moved into town, and..." He hesitated, dreading Enzo's reaction. "It does weird things."

Enzo stared blankly. "Weird things? Like what? Tap dance? Dice vegetables?"

Cooper narrowed his eyes. "Look, I know this sounds crazy, but it seems to grant wishes."

Enzo raised his eyebrows and made little effort to

suppress his amusement. "Where is it, 'cause I have a wish. I wish you made sense, but you don't."

Cooper shut his eyes and exhaled. He couldn't blame Enzo. "There's been a series of, well, let's just call them coincidences. For starters, she kind of wished me into her life." He braced for Enzo's reaction.

Enzo was surprisingly serious. He nodded, clearly reflecting. "So she wished for a nut job to come into her life."

Cooper's patience was waning. "Hey, I'm the sane one. Not that she isn't. That didn't come out right." He winced. "What I'm trying to say is that stuff happens. And I'm fine if she wants to credit the snow globe. But the thing is, I like her. If it weren't for the snow globe situation, everything would be perfect."

Enzo looked at his friend sincerely. "*Perfect* is a pretty strong word."

Cooper nodded.

"I haven't heard you use that in this context, like, ever."

"I know."

Enzo shook his head in disbelief. "I feel like we should get your shoes bronzed or something."

Cooper frowned in confusion.

"You know, baby's first love." He smiled proudly.

Cooper stared and said blandly, "Ouch. My sides."

Enzo studied Cooper. "I don't know. It's been a long time, but I seem to recall being happy when I fell in love."

"Happy? You were like a puppy with a Frisbee, just bounding around with a permanent smile."

Enzo nodded. "I was pretty happy. Still am. I'm just too tired to show it."

Cooper laughed.

"So, what are you going to do?"

Still feeling troubled, Cooper said, "Actually, we just did it."

Enzo raised his eyebrows knowingly.

Cooper grimaced in disgust. "Not that!" He rolled his eyes. "We just returned the snow globe to the store."

Enzo lifted his palms. "Great. Problem solved."

Cooper let out a weary sigh. "I don't know. That's what we're hoping, but we'll see."

Enzo leaned back. "To be honest, I don't see the problem. So she's obsessed with the snow globe. I used to be like that with cars." He sighed wistfully. "I miss those days." He stared off into the distance with a dreamy expression until his watch alarm interrupted his reverie.

Enzo glanced at the time. "Gotta go." He stood as if ready to leave then turned back. "Oh, don't forget Friday!"

With a blank stare, Cooper asked, "What's Friday?"

Enzo opened his mouth in apparent disbelief then chuckled. "Oh, you're hilarious."

Cooper grinned. "See you Friday." He waved his friend off and leaned back in his chair to ponder his Laura situation.

Laura shut the front door and leaned against it with a tired sigh. The snow globe was back in Jessica's hands, yet she didn't feel the sense of relief she'd hoped for. All day, an unsettled feeling had lingered. She kept replaying their conversation with Jessica, unable to shake her cryptic warning.

As for Cooper, the snow globe no longer loomed between them. They were free to face the future unburdened. But the future was an unanswered question. What if Cooper's feelings weren't genuine? The thought gripped her heart with fear. If she lost him, her heart would break.

With a determined exhale, Laura tried to clear her mind. It was time to dig down and move forward.

Her phone rang. For once, she was grateful for the distraction. "Hi, Mom!"

"Hi, honey! I'm in town for the day to do some Christmas shopping. Care to join me?"

Laura hesitated, glancing at her growing to-do list on the counter. "Uh, sure."

"Great! I'll pick you up in twenty minutes." Her

mother's voice held a hint of excitement that seemed a little excessive but sweet.

Once the two of them arrived in town and were wandering through the festive shops along Main Street, Laura's mother steered the conversation toward Cooper. "Delia mentioned that things are getting serious between you two," she began, holding up a sparkling ornament for inspection.

"*Serious* might be overstating it at this point, but we'll see."

"That's nice." Her mother hesitated. "We like Cooper, but when Delia told us it was serious, we were concerned."

"Concerned?" Laura echoed, feeling her heart sink. So much for a lovely day of holiday shopping with her mother.

"Your father and I just want the best for you," her mother continued, her gaze fixed on the ornament. "Cooper seems nice enough, but we don't think he's right for you."

"Really?" Laura sighed. "Well, I do."

Her mother's look made her cringe. "I know, honey, but we've always imagined you with... someone more ambitious."

Laura squinted as she tried to discern what that meant. With her mother, there was always an unspoken meaning. "I'm not sure what you mean. He's a very hard worker."

"I'm sure he is, but can he support you?"

Laura glanced at her watch. "Oh, look. It's the twenty-first century. I've been supporting myself since I got out of college." Laura held back her frustration. Her parents meant well, but their disapproval weighed on her. "Mom, it's okay. We just met. We've spent some time together. Let's not get ahead of ourselves."

Her mother placed the ornament on the shelf and sighed. "I'm not one to judge, but your father will take some convincing."

"Convincing of what? That it's okay for me to go out on a date? It's a bit late for that, don't you think?"

Her mother stared straight ahead with her mouth open as if poised to speak, but she exhaled as if giving up.

Laura glanced around then exclaimed, "Oh, look! Hot chocolate! Let's get some!"

As THE DAY WENT ON, Laura couldn't shake the doubts her mother had planted. Things weren't exactly looking up like she'd hoped. She didn't know where she stood with Cooper. Her mother and father both disapproved of the relationship. And she was falling in love.

"Look at these handmade ornaments," her mother said. "Aren't they beautiful?"

Laura nodded and forced a smile. The delicate

glass bauble shimmered as its intricate designs caught the light. It was beautiful. So were the dozens of others her mother had gushed over. The woman had an obsession with glass ornaments. Then a thought struck Laura. *Is this how Cooper felt when I brought up the snow globe?* She followed numbly along to the next ornament kiosk. A whiff of cinnamon and cloves brought her back to her senses. Hooking an arm about her mother's elbow, Laura led the way to a stand overflowing with gingerbread cookies in all shapes and sizes.

Her mother's eyes lit up with excitement. "Oh, we've got to get some of these for your father. He'll love them, don't you think?"

"How could he not?"

They selected an assortment of cookies and exchanged pleasantries with the vendor before continuing on their way.

Her mother reorganized her shopping bags and asked, "Why don't you bring some of these gingerbread cookies on Christmas Eve?"

Christmas Eve was a difficult topic that Laura had been avoiding. "Um, Mom, I've made plans."

Her mother cast sharp eyes at Laura. "Plans? For Christmas Eve?"

"Well, yes. I didn't think you'd want me to make the drive back and forth two days in a row."

Despite looking like the two trips weren't a problem, her mother showed some restraint. But over the course of a lifetime, Laura had learned to see past her mother's neutral expression to the dismay underneath.

"We assumed you'd stay over."

Laura said gently, "I've just moved in, and I'd like to enjoy Christmas Eve in my home. But I'll be there on Christmas Day."

Her mother nodded halfheartedly with a long-suffering expression that made the moment unbearable.

Laura added, "And I've got Christmas Eve plans."

Her mother frowned. "Hmm."

Laura tried to explain. "I'm building a life here."

"I can see that. It just won't be the same Christmas Eve without you."

"I'll still be there for Christmas," Laura said softly, reaching out to squeeze her mother's hand. Her mother's acquiescent nod wasn't exactly a win, but it was as much as Laura could hope for.

They continued browsing the market, sampling roasted chestnuts and admiring a colorful array of knit scarves. As the day wore on, Laura could sense her mother's disappointment still lingering beneath the surface, but neither of them spoke of it again.

When they finally parted ways, her mother handed Laura a small, beautifully wrapped package. In a voice thick with emotion, she said, "Since you won't be home for Christmas Eve, here's your Christmas Eve present to open."

"Thanks, Mom. But why don't you take it, and I can open it on Christmas Day?"

Her mother bristled, making Laura regret her words.

"It's a family tradition! We always open one gift on Christmas Eve. This is yours," her mother insisted.

"Thanks, Mom." The gesture touched her. As she gave her mother a hug, the scent of her familiar perfume enveloped Laura in a wave of nostalgia.

As they said their goodbyes, Laura clutched the gift bag and went to her front door. With a last wave as her mother drove off, Laura walked inside and glanced at the empty space on her mantel. With the move, the repairs, and her Christmas plans settled, maybe now she could build her new life.

SIXTEEN

Laura stood back and admired her handiwork. The Christmas tree sparkled with twinkling lights and shimmering ornaments, each carefully chosen to represent a cherished memory. Candles flickered in the dim room, casting warm, dancing shadows on the walls. She pulled a lasagna out of the oven, packed a tote bag with a bottle of wine, and added a stack of her all-time favorite Christmas movies and a couple of gifts.

With a few minutes to spare before leaving for Christmas Eve at Cooper's house, she settled down on the couch and wrapped a soft blanket around her shoulders. Outside, falling snow was beginning to blanket the town with wintry magic. It was just the sort of Christmas Eve she'd dreamed of—simple and serene. Laura sighed.

Then the power went out, plunging her home

into darkness. Her heart sank as the festive atmosphere vanished.

"It's okay," she muttered, rubbing her temples. "I'll just light some more candles and a fire and read until it's time to go. With any luck, the power will come back on by then."

She was about to light another candle when a knock sounded at the door. She opened it to find Cooper standing on the doorstep, his sandy blond hair dusted with snowflakes. In his hands was a white cardboard box.

"Come in." As Cooper stepped inside, a gust of wind blew out her candles and left them in darkness.

While Laura fumbled around for some matches, Cooper pulled out his phone and turned on the flashlight.

After the candles were relit, Cooper set down a white cardboard box tied with string. "These are for you."

Laura smiled. "Oh! Something smells good!" She gestured toward the box. "Shall I?"

Cooper nodded. "They're homemade cookies."

Surprised, she asked, "Did you make them?"

Cooper laughed, rubbing the back of his neck. "Uh, no. Trust me, you wouldn't want them if I had. No, they're from the bakery."

"Thank you." Their gazes lingered in the warm candlelight. Then Laura drew in a breath. "Wasn't I supposed to come to your house?"

"Yes. Sorry. I should've explained. When the power went out, I thought you might need some help over here. Let's load up and head to my house. I've got the generator running, so we can carry on with our Christmas Eve plans."

As Laura put the lasagna pan in a casserole carrier, she said, "I've had this carrier for a year with no occasion to use it. It was a gift from my mom. Apparently, she had a notion that my life involved a series of potluck dinners for singles." She looked at Cooper. "It doesn't."

They packed up and arrived minutes later at Cooper's, where the table was already set, complete with candles and wine. Over plates of lasagna and salad, they reminisced about past Christmases, joyous gatherings with friends and family, and the simple pleasures of exchanging gifts and sharing meals. The conversation was flowing easily, filling the room with a gentle and romantic ambiance, when a sudden gust rattled the windows, reminding them of the stormy reality outside.

The wind howled as if voicing a warning to stay inside for the night. Cooper said, "You might want to think about spending the night in my guest room."

While she appreciated the thought, she wasn't ready to surrender to the weather yet.

Cooper added, "I can't send you back to a home with no heat."

He had a point. "I should look into getting a generator, shouldn't I?"

Cooper tilted his head. "They come in handy." He stood and started clearing the table. "In the meantime, the offer stands."

When the dishes were cleared and the dishwasher loaded, they settled down in the living room by the fire. Laura gasped. "Oh! I almost forgot. My Christmas Eve gift."

When she saw Cooper's curious expression, she said, "It's a family tradition. My mother gave me my Christmas Eve gift, and I almost forgot to open it, so I added it to my tote bag and brought it here. If she doesn't hear from me, she'll think I hate it or that I'm in some sort of peril." She laughed.

With a sweeping gesture, Cooper said, "Bring it here. Let's see what it is."

As she unwrapped the box, Laura said, "I meant to do this at home."

Cooper shrugged. "It's Christmas Eve. What better way to spend it than by opening gifts?"

Laura gently tore off the wrapping paper, opened the flaps of the brown cardboard box, and pulled out the tissue inside. For a moment, she couldn't breathe.

"Laura? Are you okay?"

Too stunned to speak, she handed the box to Cooper.

He took one look inside. "Oh." Their eyes locked in shared shock. Inside the gift box was Laura's snow globe. Cooper took it out of the box. "It can't be the same one." But he turned it over in his hands and examined it.

Then Laura took it and did the same. "It is. It's the same one. But how?" She shook her head slightly. "My mother was in town yesterday. She must have gone into Jessica's shop before she picked me up. But how could she have known about this?" She didn't want to believe the next thought that occurred to her. "You don't suppose Jessica did this on purpose?"

Cooper shook his head slowly. "She wouldn't do that, knowing how you feel about it. Besides, how could she? She doesn't know your mother, does she?"

"No." Laura's eyes widened.

"So she couldn't have known she was selling it to your mother."

"But then... Oh my gosh! *It* did this." She couldn't stand the thought of holding it, so she handed it to Cooper. "I can't get rid of it. It's taken control."

Cooper put a comforting hand on her shoulder. "Let's not get carried away. It's just a Christmas decoration."

Laura brushed her stray hair with a trembling hand. "A Christmas decoration that's controlling my life!"

"Hey. It's okay."

She searched his eyes, wanting so much to believe him. "You don't understand."

"Then help me."

She considered it for a moment, but when she glanced at him, he looked so warm and caring that she forged ahead. "I have worked so hard to maintain control of my life. It's how I've managed to cope all these years."

Cooper narrowed his eyes in confusion.

"You've seen my sister's friends. A lifetime of their ridicule taught me to control what I could. Have you not noticed what a control freak I am?"

Cooper hesitated, looking more diplomatic than indecisive. "Well, now that you mention it..."

"It's okay. I know it's a little out there."

A hint of amusement lit his eyes. "Doesn't everyone uniformly fold and sort microfiber towels by color? Everyone except me, that is."

"I know." His smile was so warm and kind that she didn't mind his amusement. "But it makes me feel better when everything is where it should be." She drew in a breath and sighed. "I can relax. That's what I love about accounting. There are rules. Things balance, and that gives me peace." She shrugged helplessly. Either he would understand, or he would think she was a little nutty. Either way, it was best for him to know now.

His eyes softened. "Come here." He set down the snow globe and drew Laura into his arms. "It's okay."

She didn't believe him for a minute, but his strong embrace comforted her.

He lifted her chin and looked into her eyes. "Don't worry. We'll figure out this snow globe thing."

Laura nodded, not because she believed him but because she wanted to.

He smiled. "That explains our first meeting. Until then, I'd never seen perfectly matched and stacked moving boxes. It was... impressive."

"I'm surprised you noticed, what with half of the ceiling tangled in my hair."

His eyes sparkled. "One piece of drywall."

Laura chuckled. "A very large piece!"

"But you wore it with panache."

The warmth in his eyes nearly convinced her that everything would be all right. Then her gaze would fall to the snow globe, and the knot in her stomach would tighten.

Apparently seeing her eyes fixed on the snow globe, Cooper said, "We could pack it away in a lead box."

Laura laughed. "I guess that could work—for Superman. Since this isn't kryptonite, I'm not sure how effective that would be."

"Oh, I don't know. You haven't seen me in a blue spandex bodysuit and red cape."

"No, that's true." Laura took a moment to imagine it. "Moving on. What if we... buried it in the backyard?"

He narrowed his eyes. "Like a dead body?"

Laura shrugged. "In a tiny round coffin."

Cooper shook his head.

Laura bit her lip. "We could go deep-sea fishing and drop it into the ocean."

Cooper lifted his eyebrows. "Too bad it's the offseason." He stared at the snow globe. "This is going to sound a little crazy, but why not just return it?"

"Again? I've already returned it once. I can't do that to Jessica."

Cooper shook his head. "Fine, then the charity shop."

Laura nodded, approving. "That would work. Okay. The charity shop, it is."

Cooper lifted the snow globe. "Until then, let's just move this out of sight." He set it down on the sofa table behind them. "There. It feels better already, doesn't it?"

Laura wrinkled her face. "Sort of."

"It's a start."

Laura couldn't let it go. "I still can't believe it. That my mother of all people should give that to me. It's so out of character. Ornaments, yes. She's obsessed with them. In fact, until I opened it, I was sure that's what was in the box. We get an ornament every Christmas Eve, which is lovely. My sister and I have these collections of beautiful ornaments."

Cooper said, "So why would she suddenly depart from tradition?"

"Exactly!" A surge of frustration came out in a broad,

sweeping gesture. The back of her hand struck the snow globe. Time seemed to slow as it tumbled through the air, snow swirling, and struck the hardwood floor with a crash. The delicate pieces scattered like stars across a dark sky, as if their fractured reflections could mirror the fragile state of her relationship with Cooper. The strange, otherworldly aura that had once radiated from the globe was gone, leaving a sense of loss in its place.

Laura leapt to her feet and stood staring.

"Are you okay?" Cooper rushed to her side, his eyes wide with concern.

"Oh my gosh!" she whispered, tears pricking at the corners of her eyes. "I didn't mean to—"

"Hey, it's just a snow globe," he tried to reassure her, but his words felt hollow when shards of enchantment lay at their feet.

Laura stared at the broken remnants. "For every action, there is an equal and opposite reaction."

Cooper eyed her doubtfully. "Okay, laws of motion. Got it. But if we're going to talk Newton, maybe his law of gravity might be more fitting."

How can he joke at a time like this? "Don't you get it? I broke the snow globe, and there will be consequences!"

Looking concerned, Cooper said gently, "The only consequence will be cleaning it up." He went to the kitchen then returned moments later with a broom and dustpan.

Unable to watch, Laura paced in front of the fire-place. "I'm sorry."

Cooper glanced up. "It's fine. I've got this."

"I was talking to the snow globe."

Cooper froze for a moment then finished sweeping up the glass.

Laura stopped pacing and followed Cooper to the kitchen while he threw away the last of the pieces. She grabbed his arm and whispered, "Don't you see? The snow globe brought us together, and now that it's broken, we're broken, or we will be soon enough."

She could see in his eyes that he thought she had lost it, but she was sure that the fractures in the glass were symbolic of deeper fissures to come in their relationship. Already, Cooper had abandoned his efforts to reassure and comfort her. Instead, they stood in silence amid the ruins of what could have been a magical night, leaving Laura to wonder if the enchantment that had once bound them together was already lost.

Laura glanced around the dimly lit room, her breath catching in her chest as she struggled to hold back her tears. "Maybe this was all just a fantasy and it never was real."

Cooper's face fell, hurt flickering in his eyes. "Laura, you can't possibly believe that." He took a step closer. "Yes, the snow globe played a part in our story, but it wasn't the foundation of our relationship.

And I'm sorry, but it just wasn't magic. It was—is —real."

"Is that really true, though?" Laura had a desperate edge to her voice. "Or is it just what we want to believe?"

"Of course it's true!" Cooper insisted, his voice firm yet gentle. "You know I've been here for you since we met, since before the snow globe came into our lives. And I thought you felt the same."

"There wasn't a time before the snow globe for us. It's always been there. That's how we met." Laura shook her head, the weight of her frustration bearing down on her. "It's our foundation, and I've broken it."

"Objects don't make or break relationships."

"I hear what you're saying, and logically, it makes sense. But this has gone way beyond logic. I can't even believe I just said that, but that's how much this has shaken my world." She wasn't sure how to read Cooper's expression except that he looked gravely serious.

"Laura..." He looked down thoughtfully. "There's a lot going on. You've just moved. You're changing jobs. And as much as we like to think of the holidays as happy, they can be stressful and emotional."

"Great. So you think I'm too emotional?" She wanted to leave and avoid what was bound to come next. But the storm howled outside as if to remind her that she couldn't go home yet.

"No. I just think there's a lot going on."

"So, you want to break up?" She paused then looked up. "Are we even together? I don't want to assume."

He put his hands on her shoulders. "Slow down. Let's just give it some time."

"It?"

"Us." He was practically smiling, which Laura took as a flicker of hope.

Maybe Cooper was right. Maybe love was strong enough to weather the storm and mend the fractures that had formed between them.

"Give it some time?" Her heart pounded in her chest as she tried to imagine it.

He gently said, "Yes."

He was so impressively calm, and she wasn't. She heaved a sigh. "Maybe you're right."

"Let's start by picking up the pieces, and I'm not talking figuratively." His eyes lit up with amusement, as if life were really that simple. He reached out and gave her hand a squeeze. "I'll grab the broom. You do the dustpan."

And that should have been it, except Laura couldn't let it go. She had the same feeling she got when books wouldn't balance. In her job, everything had a solution. Even when she couldn't find it, she knew it was there. She just had to persist.

She followed Cooper to the kitchen while he emptied the dustpan. "The thing is, how can we know it was real?" Part of her knew she should have left things alone, but fear gnawed at her. "It's always going to be in the back of my mind."

"There's no way you'll believe that my feelings are real?" Cooper's voice sounded tense with frustration. "So everything we've shared was just an illusion?"

"Maybe." Laura fought back her emotions. "And I just broke it."

He narrowed his eyes and stared off into the distance. "First, you should know me well enough to know I'm not much of a follower. Second, even if I were, I wouldn't take romantic cues from inanimate objects."

Laura opened her mouth, but before she could speak, Cooper continued. "Third, I've told you how I feel. The fact that I'm still here should confirm it." Cooper shut his eyes as if summoning patience. "If this were anyone else, I'd be gone."

"Except this is your house, so I guess I'd be gone." With a sudden realization, she said, "Oh. I should go."

He seemed genuinely alarmed. "No!" He ran his fingers through his hair in frustration. "Is it me? Am I just not speaking clearly enough? I mean, obviously not. Look, I'm trying to tell you I love you!"

He looked as surprised as she did. Laura couldn't move or speak.

He took a few breaths to calm down. "Sorry. That wasn't how I meant to share that bit of news. I wasn't planning to say it at all. It's too early. It's not the sort of thing you say at this point in our relationship. Sorry."

"You're sorry you love me?"

He frowned, rubbing his forehead. "No, I'm sorry I blurted it out like an awkward adolescent. I just mean I don't need a snow globe to tell me I love you."

"Then why does it feel like everything is falling apart?" Laura demanded, her voice cracking. "Why do I feel like I'm losing you?"

"Because you're letting your fear get the best of you." The edge in his voice revealed how thin his patience was. "Look, I get it. The snow globe is a sort of symbol for you—your big move, your new life. It's a loss. But it's only an object. It doesn't define us or our relationship unless we let it. We've got to trust each other and ourselves."

"Trust?" Laura scoffed, her heart heavy with doubt. "How can I trust anything when our entire relationship was built on something that wasn't real?"

Cooper yelled, "Laura! Can you hear yourself?"

Laura flinched. She had never seen him lose his temper like that.

Cooper turned away and took a deep breath. "Sorry. I'm sorry. Look, there's nothing more I can say. It doesn't matter how I feel because you have some things to work out."

"Cooper, I..." Laura faltered, her mind a whirlwind of conflicted emotions. She whispered, "I should go." She went to the door and pulled her coat from a hook. Outside, the snow flew as the wind tossed it about, but she couldn't stay any longer.

"Wait, Laura! Don't go. It's not safe!" Cooper pleaded, reaching for her arm.

Shaking off his touch, she pulled on her gloves. "No, you're right. I need to figure things out on my own, and I can't do that here."

And with that, Laura stepped out into the storm, leaving Cooper and her broken snow globe behind.

Once outside, Laura realized she hadn't driven over there. Cooper had. But she wasn't about to go back inside. Besides, it was just a few blocks from her house. So she started walking. The frigid wind whipped her, chilling her to the bone as she trudged through the thick layer of snow blanketing Cooper's yard. She'd come dressed to walk out to the truck, not to tromp through knee-deep snow. She envisioned her parka and fleece-lined boots in the closet and desperately missed them. With each step, icy snow breached the tops of her ankle-high boots while the biting cold found its way past her collar and up through her sleeves.

Barely able to see past the flying snowflakes ahead, she allowed her mind to race with conflicting thoughts and emotions. Could it truly be love, or was she just dreaming of what Christmas could be? When had she lost track of logic?

COOPER STOOD in the doorway and watched the woman he loved head down the driveway, ignoring his calls. "Damn it," he muttered under his breath, clenching his fists. She could hate him all she wanted, and she probably did, but he was going to see her safely home. He pulled on his jacket and headed for his truck.

Laura had barely made it a block by the time he pulled up beside her and opened the door. "Get in."

The fact that she took him up on the offer so quickly was a testament to the storm's fierceness. The two-minute drive to her house felt much longer in the silence.

He pulled into the driveway. "I wish you'd reconsider. You don't have any heat."

"I've got a fireplace. It was good enough for the pioneers."

"The pioneers might have been cold."

"I'll be fine."

"If you change your mind, call me anytime. I'll have the phone by my bed. I can be here in two minutes."

With a simple thank-you, she got out of the truck and went into her house.

SEVENTEEN

The Christmas morning sunlight cast a sparkling sheen on the snow-blanketed front yards outside. The world was pristine and serene, a picture-perfect street scene that belied Laura's tumultuous emotions still lingering from the night before.

She sat by the window in her parents' warm house, cradling a mug of steaming coffee between her hands. Outside, children bundled up in colorful scarves and hats tumbled into the snow, their laughter ringing through the crisp air. Parents on doorsteps watched their children and called out well-wishes for the holiday season to one another. The joy would have been contagious if it hadn't amplified the emptiness she felt inside.

"Beautiful morning, isn't it?" Her mother's voice pulled Laura from her thoughts, but she couldn't bring herself to respond with more than a "hmm." Instead, she continued to gaze out the window, her hazel eyes clouded with regret.

"Sweetheart, I know you're upset about last night," Pamela said gently, sitting down beside her daughter. "But dwelling on it won't change anything."

Laura sighed, unable to shake the memories of the shattered snow globe and her argument with Cooper. "I know, but it's not really a choice. It's like being run over by a truck then trying not to dwell on the pain. Except I'm the truck too. I've ruined everything, Mom." She cast her a sideways look and added, "Including your gift."

"Everyone makes mistakes," Pamela reassured her. "What matters is how we learn from them and move forward." Her mother had a seemingly endless supply of aphorisms that made perfect sense and yet didn't help one bit.

"By moving forward, I hope you mean with Cooper. I know you had some concerns, but once you get to know him, you'll see what an amazing person he is."

Her mom nodded, though her expression was doubtful. "I'm sure he is."

An awkward silence hung in the air. Laura knew her parents meant well, but their disapproval of Cooper stung.

Outside, the children had begun building snow-men, their cheeks flushed pink from the cold. Laura envied their carefree spirits. If only she could erase the previous night and start over, but the memory haunted her.

"I should apologize to him," Laura mused aloud. "I let my feelings override logic, which just isn't like me. I haven't been myself since..." Her voice trailed off as she thought of the snow globe. *No, I will not go there again.* At some point during her sleepless night, she'd decided the topic would be off-limits. Cooper was right. It was only an object. In the midst of her dreams and expectations for Christmas, she'd allowed the snow globe's importance to grow out of proportion.

"I don't know what came over me. Emotional roller coasters just aren't my thing. And poor Cooper. He tried." She picked up her phone and set it back down again. "He's probably at his mother's by now. I should let them enjoy Christmas and save this for later."

Pamela gave her daughter's hand a comforting squeeze. "Remember, the magic of Christmas can't be found in decorations and presents. It's in your heart."

Laura offered a mechanical nod but paused as she realized her mother might actually have a good point. Laura had spent so much time and energy on her new home in her perfect small town that she hadn't given much thought to the meaning of Christmas. Her thoughts were so full of Cooper, she wondered if there was room left for anything else. As for Cooper's feelings, she feared she'd destroyed them along with the snow globe. And yet, as she thought over the previous evening, she recalled Cooper's kindness, his patience, and regrettably, his concern. None of that could have come from the snow globe. It was too much a part of him. It was clear that it came from his heart. She would have seen that if she'd trusted him.

"Thanks, Mom," she said softly.

With a quick hug, her mother said, "Now then, I've got some cookies to bake!"

Laura's smile faded as her mother headed for the kitchen. If only her parents could see Cooper as she did. His actions revealed a depth of character that she'd seldom encountered.

Still, expecting her parents' opinion of him to shift overnight was unrealistic. But if she gently but consistently emphasized Cooper's merits and gave them opportunities to see who he truly was, in time, they would come around. She hoped.

COOPER SIGHED as he wrapped the cord around the vacuum cleaner, his jaw set with determination. Busying himself with Christmas morning chores wasn't distracting him from thoughts of his argument with Laura. It was futile. Every thought seemed to lead back to her—the Christmas Eve cookies sitting untouched on the kitchen counter, the small stack of holiday movies he'd envisioned them watching together, and even the vacuuming to catch any last bits of glass that had escaped the earlier cleanup. Rather than serving as a distraction, the cleanup effort was a painful reminder of what he had lost.

"Maybe I was too harsh," Cooper muttered under his breath, staring at the empty space on the table where the snow globe had sat. "Could I have handled things differently?" The question gnawed at him.

As if in response, a gust of wind blew through the town of Mistletoe, swirling icy crystals of snow against the windows. In the storm's aftermath, the world outside appeared pristine and untroubled. An occasional car passed by, probably carrying a family to their Christmas festivities. Soon, he would head to his mother's house for their usual quiet, content Christmas dinner. It was one of the constants in life— spending Christmas with family. Traditions gave life its center. But in the wake of his evening with Laura, his life felt off-balance.

He loved her. How had that happened? It wasn't magic. That much he knew. It certainly wasn't because of a silly snow globe. He loved her because she was Laura—because from the moment she'd opened the door with bits of drywall and dust in her hair, his world had shifted.

He caught sight of himself in a mirror. "Now look at yourself." He moaned.

Cooper shook off his mood and got ready to go. After filling the car with an armload of gifts, he headed for his mother's house. On the way, he made his usual stop at Enzo's.

"Coop! Come on in!" Enzo's home was a chaotic scene of torn wrapping paper, toys, and video games.

Cooper handed a couple of gift bags to Enzo and stood by the door. "I can't stay. I'm on my way to my mom's, but I just wanted to drop these off."

"Thanks, man. Come in. At least have a cup of coffee." He leaned closer and beckoned. "It's a little quieter in the kitchen. Come on."

Cooper hesitated for a second then followed. After hugs for Enzo's wife and the kids, Cooper escaped to the kitchen with his friend. Cooper sat while Enzo poured them each a mug of coffee and sat down. After Enzo gave Cooper a rundown of his family's Christmas, the talk turned to Cooper. He managed to condense the previous evening into a few sentences and a shrug.

Enzo listened intently, his brow furrowing. "Look," he said finally, setting a palm on the table. "I'm not going to lie. Love is a miserable endeavor. It's also the best thing that's ever happened to me. For instance, last night, I lost half a night's sleep putting together that friggin' pile of toys out there. Was it fun? No. Did the kids get up and nearly catch me at it three times, wanting glasses of water and looking for Santa? Yes. Is my wife completely exhausted, even though she's got a full morning of cooking ahead, and are our families due in a couple of hours? Yes." He looked straight at Cooper and grinned. "And I wouldn't give this up for anything."

"I envy you."

Enzo blew air through his lips. "That's not why I told you all that. My point is that love isn't about skipping in slow motion through a meadow with the lady you love. Don't get me wrong. We still manage to frolic now and then, if you know what I mean. But the rest of the time, stuff happens. Love happens. Once you accept it, add another person to the mix. It's like finding your balance again."

"Yeah, well, sometimes you don't. You just fall on your face."

Enzo smirked. "Not you. You'll be fine. So will she. You just have to decide whether to be fine together."

Cooper narrowed his eyes. "You make it sound simple."

From the other room came the voices of arguing children. Enzo burst out laughing. "Hear that? That's love."

Cooper grinned. "I'd better let you get back to your family."

They stood and headed to the door. A round of

hugs and handshakes later, Enzo said, "Give my best to your mom."

"I will, and my best to your parents."

As Cooper headed outside to his car, Enzo yelled, "Call her!"

Without looking back, Cooper waved, but that didn't mean he was going to do it.

EIGHTEEN

It was dark when Laura arrived home from Christmas Day with her family. The house lights were on, so the power was back. As she unloaded the trunk of her car and headed inside, she remembered how Cooper had insisted they go through the house and turn off any light switches and faucets that were on when the power went out. They'd obviously missed one or two.

With a pang in her heart, she recalled how happy they had been while getting ready to go to his house for Christmas Eve. Her family's Christmas festivities had helped keep thoughts of Cooper at bay, but now that she was home, heartache overwhelmed her.

A gust of wind blew an icy mist at her face, and she shivered. There was no avoiding her feelings, so she would confront them. That called for a mug of hot cocoa and a Christmas movie—something that said, "It's a miserable life." She would start by watching Judy Garland sing "Have Yourself a Merry Little Christmas" while she looked on the internet, the source of all wisdom, for a list of the saddest Christmas movies of all time.

Love Actually came to mind. She was easily as sad as the Laura Linney and Emma Thompson characters, not to mention the guy with the signs. It was a shame the stores were all closed. Although Cooper had mentioned that one of her neighbors was an elementary school teacher, which meant she was bound to have stockpiles of markers and poster board. Laura would have to embark upon a new career as a cat burglar, but tough times called for tough measures.

I could ring Cooper's doorbell and stand holding my posters. Perfect. There. A well-defined action plan always makes everything better. What would I write on the posters?

Hey, Cooper,
How do I look standing here with these cards?

Don't answer that.
The thing is, I'm here because...

Err...

Just because it's Christmas,

And at Christmas, it used to be customary...

To go door-to-door and harass people with song.

Lucky for you, I'm not singing.
(Have you heard me sing?)

No... I'm just standing here because...
Christmas is a magical time, and

Even though the snow globe made you do it,
I loved how you seemed to love me,
Because...

I love you.
(Sad face)

So, Merry Christmas.
Oh, and—I hate to ask,

But could you take a look at my faucet? It's leaking.
Sorry, but you're the only handyman in town.

Merry Christmas...
Walking away now.

How many cards would I need for all that? Too

many, even for a teacher. I'd have to break into a church's Sunday school classroom.

She turned the key in her front-door lock, stepped inside, locked the door, and hung her coat on a hook.

"Laura?"

Laura screamed and practically levitated out of her fur-trimmed boots. "Cooper! What are you doing here? You can't just break into people's houses!"

His dog, Duke, whose large paws seemed almost too big for his body, skidded slightly along the wooden floor as he rounded the corner from the kitchen to greet Laura. She bent down and gave Duke a neck rub then looked up at Cooper.

"I didn't break in. Well, technically, maybe. But— sorry. I was out walking Duke, and I saw you weren't home, so I—"

"Thought you'd break in and—"

With a wry look, he said, "There's a key over the doorframe."

"Not for you!"

"Laura, anyone wanting to break in would check the doormat, a potted plant, and the doorframe. It's not exactly Fort Knox."

"So you're here for a home security check?"

He calmly said, "No..."

"Cooper, you scared the stuffing out of me!"

"Sorry. I assumed you'd be staying overnight at your parents', so I wanted to check to make sure we didn't accidentally leave a random faucet or stove on when the power went out."

"Oh." Realizing he meant well, she relaxed, but her frown was still fading when she said, "Thanks. That was thoughtful."

He lifted his shoulders, which could have meant it was nothing or that he wished he'd never stopped by at all. She imagined that from now on he would walk his dog in the other direction.

Laura could have gone on imagining since neither one of them spoke. They just stared. Even Duke was unusually quiet.

At last, Cooper said, "I should go."

"How was your Christmas?"

He looked confused by the question. "Fine. How was yours?"

"Merry."

He looked even more confused. "Was it?"

"No."

Cooper seemed to brighten at the thought of her unmerry Christmas.

"Mine wasn't either."

"I'm sorry."

He asked, "About my Christmas or yours?"

She nodded. "Both. And last night."

His gaze softened, which completely undid any hope Laura had of holding back her emotions. Cooper held out his arms. "Come here."

She sank into his embrace and buried her face in

his neck. All she wanted for Christmas was to lean into the warmth of his chest with his strong arms around her. It was a perfect moment.

When he loosened his arms and leaned back, he put his hands on her shoulders. "Nothing's changed from last night."

There went her perfect moment.

He gazed into her eyes. "I still feel the same about you."

With a sigh, she let out tension she hadn't realized she was holding in.

Cooper's narrowed eyes didn't bode well for what was coming next. "But..."

Laura braced herself.

Cooper paused midsentence. "Let's sit down. First, let's turn on the heat."

While he adjusted the thermostat, Laura turned on the gas fireplace, then she sat on the sofa, holding her knees, and he joined her.

After a few seconds of silence, Cooper began. "I've been thinking."

"Me too." *Borderline obsessing. No, just plain obsessing.*

His penetrating gaze wasn't easy to take. She couldn't tell whether he was angry, fed up, or worse, disappointed in her. After all, a grown woman—a usually logical woman—should be able to put things like snow globes into perspective.

When he showed no sign of speaking, Laura said,

"Look, I still don't understand everything that has happened, but I do understand that I need to trust you."

"Not just me—your own feelings." He added, "For me. If you have them."

"Of course I have feelings for you! Maybe it's because it—we—happened too easily." She fixed her eyes on the floor. "I didn't understand how you could..."

"Care for you?" His soft gaze nearly melted her heart. "How could I not?"

She lifted her eyes to meet his. "Because I'm... me?"

"But that's what I love about you." He shook his head. "Laura." His gaze trailed to her lips, and he kissed her. "I told you how I feel about you." He kissed her again. "But we can't build a relationship with a snow globe between us."

"I know."

"Do you?"

With all her heart, she said, "Yes."

His eyes searched hers. "Are you sure?"

With a nod, she leaned back. "I know I got caught up in a dream of my new home and the perfect Christmas town. The snow globe, magic or not, was a part of it all. When I looked into that globe, I saw my house, this town, and the small-town Christmas I'd dreamed of."

Cooper looked troubled. "Mistletoe is a town like

any other town. Yes, it's charming when we've fixed it all up for the holidays. But towns are made up of people, just like cities. We're not perfect. We're just people. And the feelings we have don't come from any sort of Christmas magic."

"I know, but it all seemed so unbelievably perfect."

He took her hand in both of his. "No, it's just real. I'm asking you to trust that."

"I do."

He went on. "Because, God forbid, any manner of natural disaster could flatten the town tomorrow and destroy all of its holiday charm. But the people would pull together and rebuild the town, because it's the people who make up a small town. The picturesque buildings along Main Street and the little village in your snow globe are just things."

"I know that now."

"If you want Christmas magic, just look in your heart. The real magic is there."

Laura's breath caught in her chest as Cooper's intense blue eyes bored into hers. His strong hands gripped her shoulders, holding her fast. Her pulse quickened.

"Laura..." Cooper's husky voice sent shivers down her spine. Unable to resist any longer, Laura crushed her mouth to his in a scorching kiss.

Cooper responded with equal fervor. She arched toward him, every nerve in her body electric and alive, and clung to him as though he were her lifeline, the only solid thing in a dizzying world.

At last, they broke away, catching their breath. As she gazed up at Cooper's smoldering eyes, Laura knew she was lost—hopelessly and utterly lost to that man.

A light came to his eyes as he drew closer and kissed her. "Besides, I'm a way better kisser than that guy in your snow globe."

Laura laughed.

"If I'm not, lie and tell me I am."

"I never kissed him 'cause that would've been weird. You're the only man in Mistletoe I've kissed."

He took her face in his hands. "Good. Let's keep it that way." Then he kissed her.

NINETEEN

THE FIRST LIGHT of morning cast long shadows on the snow-covered lawns in the village. Laura rose from her bed, drawn to the window by the shimmering beauty outside. Shivering slightly, she pulled on her robe, feeling the cold seep through the windowpane.

"Such a perfect day," she whispered, her breath fogging the glass.

Her phone chimed with a text, and she smiled to see it was from Cooper.

Cooper: How does a diner breakfast sound?

Laura: Perfect.

Cooper: Thirty minutes? (I'm starving!)

Laura: Okay. See you then!

She didn't have to ask where. There was one diner in town that looked as though it had traveled through time from the 1950s. Laura couldn't think of a more perfect place for a leisurely post-Christmas breakfast. After a quick shower, she pulled on her most lived-in jeans and an oversized sweater, wrapped a scarf around her neck, and donned her outdoor gear. It was so pretty outside that she decided to walk. A few flurries floated aimlessly about as she made her way along the side streets that led into town.

By the time she arrived, Cooper was settled in a booth with two coffees. His face lit up when he saw her, as hers must have. She couldn't help staring. Realizing she must have a ridiculous grin on her face, she averted her eyes and slid into the booth. They said good morning and seemed stuck in the same blissful yet noncommunicative state.

Cooper looked down at the table with a half-embarrassed smile. "I know this sounds a little pathetic since it's only been hours, but I missed you."

When he lifted his eyes to meet Laura's, her heart skipped a beat. "It doesn't sound pathetic. It sounds perfect."

He slowly nodded as if deep in thought. "You know what that means."

Laura didn't have a clue, so Cooper explained. "It means we're both pathetic, but I hope in a good way."

Laura tucked one leg under her knee and leaned on the table. "I'm fine with being pathetic. As for being hungry..."

"I know! Hold on." He glanced around, caught

the server's eye, and gave a wave with such a charming smile that, in her place, Laura would have ignored every other table and rushed to serve him.

Minutes later, they were digging into omelets, home fries, and toast. After he'd sated his ravenous appetite, Cooper dropped his fork on the plate. "Is there anything better than this?" He quickly added, "I mean, there might be a few things, but this is pretty darn good."

"A day off, a diner breakfast, and nothing to do in the world but enjoy it? Absolutely!"

Cooper took another bite. "Well, I do have something in mind."

Laura raised her eyebrows and waited.

All Cooper would say was "After breakfast."

Laura felt thoroughly at ease for a change. The conversation was light and often lapsed into comfortable silence. She leaned back and observed the comings and goings around them. People entered, and the two of them almost always knew someone to greet with holiday wishes. No one seemed in a rush. Of course, it was a holiday week. Still, there was a warmth that Laura had never known in her neighborhood back home.

Laura tried to pay the check, but Cooper insisted on taking care of it himself. Once outside, Laura paused. "You mentioned you had something in mind. Did you mean now, later, or next Christmas?"

He laughed. "Do you have any plans?"

Laura drew her eyebrows together and appeared to be thinking. "No, my schedule is pretty open today."

Looking pleased and a little relieved, Cooper said, "Good. Come with me." Then he stopped. "You're not parked at a meter, are you?"

"No, I walked."

"Perfect. I'm around the corner." He took her hand, making her wish she wasn't wearing gloves, and they walked that way until they got to his truck.

"Are you going to tell me where we're going?"

"Yes." He helped Laura into the truck then walked around and got in on the driver's side. After starting the truck and turning on the heat, he faced Laura, looking suddenly serious. "I know we worked through a lot last night, and I think—I hope—we're in a good place."

Laura nodded. "I think so."

He put his hands on the steering wheel and stared straight ahead. "I've been a little frustrated—not with you. Not to bring up a sore subject, but I couldn't find the words to explain my inherent objection to this magic snow globe situation."

Laura's heart sank. "I'm letting that go. But I did have a thought. Maybe the snow globe broke because we didn't need it anymore."

From the look on his face, that hadn't helped. Cooper was quiet for a very long couple of moments. "I want to show you something. Let's go on a tour of the real Mistletoe." He started the truck, and he drove away from the postcard-perfect section of town to some outlying neighborhoods where the tourists didn't go. "Don't get me wrong. I love the Mistletoe that people come to visit." He glanced at her and added, "The Mistletoe you moved here to live in. It's a perfect Christmas village. We all love it, but what I'm going to show you now is the heart and the soul of our town. This is the Mistletoe that I missed when I lived in the city. It's the town I want you to love. It's where I want to live for the rest of my life."

As they drove along, lights twinkled from the edges of snow-dusted rooftops and outlined picture windows, but Cooper began to paint an entirely different picture of his hometown.

"You see that woman over there, Mrs. Jennings?" He gestured to an elderly lady wrapping a scarf around a young boy's neck. "She lost her husband during the first wave of Covid, then the lockdown destroyed her son's family business. He and his family have moved in with her. Every Sunday, their neighbors and friends take turns bringing groceries and meals to help them get by until things get better."

Laura followed Cooper's gaze to a teenage boy helping his younger siblings build a snowman. "That's Kyle. His world turned upside down when the schools closed and they switched to remote learning. He was struggling with suicidal thoughts, but a group of classmates and parents rallied around him.

They set up virtual hangouts, games, and movie nights, found him some counseling, and created a support system that saw him through."

They drove past a mother and her teenage daughter delivering newspapers. "That's Tina and Molly," Cooper said. "They were just getting by when inflation sent their household expenses soaring. Tina was already working two jobs, and it still wasn't enough. So Molly quit the basketball team and took a job after school. Together, they're making it work."

Next, they drove by the back of a church where a sign read Mistletoe Food Pantry. "That elderly man unloading boxes from a truck is Mr. Henderson. He once confided in me that he did okay in the stock market a few years ago, so he gives a chunk of his social security check and a lot of free time to the food pantry. He's vowed that no child will go hungry on his watch."

A little farther down, Laura saw a young man and a middle-aged woman walking along the sidewalk.

"We're a small town, but things happen. With the police department short-staffed and crime rising, Pine Street formed a neighborhood watch to make sure everyone feels safe."

Laura's eyes filled with compassion. "It's so real," she whispered.

Cooper pulled over and parked. His gaze softened. "Yeah. It's the real Christmas magic."

Laura's eyes swept over the scene before her. It was a lot to absorb.

"Real life might not always be Christmas-card-perfect, but the spirit of this town, the way we rally behind each other—that is what makes this town special."

With a deep breath, Laura whispered to herself, "Life isn't about perfect moments. It's about the imperfect moments and how we face them together."

Cooper smiled gently. "There's a possibility you and I might have future disagreements." His eyes twinkled as a smile lit his face. "But we'll figure it out."

He gave her hand a squeeze then turned to take the wheel and pull onto the road. "So that's my hometown, and I'm glad you're a part of it."

"Me too."

New Year's Eve arrived with a flurry of excitement and anticipation as Mistletoe prepared to bid farewell to the old year and welcome a new one with open arms. In the twilight, the town square transformed into a bustling hub of activity as families and friends gathered for a fireworks display.

Laura stood beside Cooper, her hair brushing against his shoulder as they gazed up at the indigo sky, waiting for the first burst of color to announce the new year's arrival. The surrounding air crackled with energy, a palpable sense of hope and promise that mirrored the emotions in their own hearts.

As fireworks lit up the night sky, Cooper pulled Laura close, their eyes meeting for a brief moment before they sealed their newfound love with a passionate kiss.

"Happy New Year," he whispered, his breath warm against her ear.

"Happy New Year," she replied, the taste of his lips still lingering on hers.

And as the night sky filled with glittering light, Laura and Cooper stood poised to face the new year. With hearts full of hope and determination, they embraced the unknown, ready to make the most of every moment in the coming new year. They now knew that the true magic of Christmas lasted throughout the year because the true magic of Christmas was love.

EPILOGUE

ELEVEN MONTHS Later

Christmas cheer was beginning to wrap its festive arms around the quaint village of Mistletoe. In the heart of town, Jessica Carmichael stood behind the counter of her thriving antiques store, her silver hair glinting in the twinkling lights adorning the shop.

"Another magical Christmas season is upon us," she murmured to herself, a nostalgic glimmer gracing her deep-blue eyes as she thought back on Laura and the enchanting snow globe she'd sold her almost a year ago. It felt like only yesterday that Laura had walked into her store, drawn by the captivating aura of an intricately crafted snow globe. Jessica wondered what the current season would bring. She smiled as she sorted the new inventory that had arrived earlier that day. Her fingers brushed against something cold and familiar. Her face lit up with anticipation when she came to a familiar box containing another unique hand-blown snow globe. It was remarkably similar to last year's but featured a different house nestled within its glassy confines.

Earlier in the day, the mysterious white-haired craftsman had stopped by as he did once a year with a single snow globe. She still didn't get very much conversation out of him, but that morning, he'd offered an enigmatic smile and cryptic words that still echoed in her thoughts. "It's a hobby. I like to think I put a little Christmas magic in each one."

"Who could this one be for?" she wondered aloud, her curiosity piqued.

The door chimes jingled, interrupting her musings. In walked a petite young woman with short, stylish blond hair and wrapped in a thick green scarf, her cheeks rosy from the chilly winter air.

"Sandra! Hello!" Jessica stopped what she was doing to give Sandra a hug.

"Hi, Jessica." She offered her usual bright, cheery facade that masked her true feelings, or so Jessica suspected. She sensed the weight of the past year on Sandra's shoulders—the loss of her job, the year-old breakup with Cooper that she couldn't seem to get past, and the move home when her life in the city had seemed to crumble beneath her.

"It's so good to see you!"

Sandra attempted a weak smile. "Thanks."

Jessica glanced at a stack of boxes. "Look at me, chatting away like I have nothing to do. I'll let you get on with some shopping while I unpack and shelve these new items."

As Sandra wandered through the familiar aisles of the shop, her eyes fell upon the snow globe Jessica had left on the counter. Drawing closer, she gently cradled the globe in her hands, charmed by the wintry world it contained. With a wistful sigh, she carefully set it back down and worked her way up and down the aisles until she returned to the snow globe.

She called out to Jessica, who was at the end of the counter, scanning barcodes. "I don't know why I'm asking. I'm sure I can't afford it, but how much is this?"

Seeing Sandra's face glowing with childlike joy, Jessica shocked even herself by saying, "As a matter of fact, it's on sale."

"Really? So early? But Christmas isn't for another couple of weeks."

"It must be fate." Jessica had a sudden sense that it was.

"How much is it?" Sandra asked softly, her eyes still fixed on the scene within the glass sphere.

"Forty-five dollars." *Forty-five dollars? Have you lost your mind?* It had to be magic. How else could she explain selling the snow globe at cost?

Sandra shook her head slowly then shrugged. "It

must be the Christmas spirit or something. I have no business buying this, but... I'll take it."

Jessica took it and wrapped it in paper. "It must be meant for you."

Sandra pulled some bills from her wallet and combined them. "You know I wait tables in the diner, right?"

Jessica nodded.

"This morning, a man I've never seen before left me a fifty-dollar tip. I guess it must have been burning a hole in my pocket because here I am."

Jessica finished wrapping the snow globe, placed it in a red shopping bag, and handed it to Sandra. "I'm told there's a bit of Christmas magic in each one of these snow globes."

Sandra glanced around. "Oh, are there others?"

"Oh no. There's only one every year, and this year, you got it."

Sandra smiled. "Lucky for me!"

Jessica nodded. "Merry Christmas!"

"Thank you. Merry Christmas!"

By the time the little shop bell rang and Sandra was gone, Jessica realized she couldn't remember seeing Sandra that cheerful. She was glad for any part she'd played in her happiness.

With renewed Christmas cheer, Jessica turned and continued shelving her holiday inventory, wondering what sort of magical story was waiting to unfold for Sandra. It seemed the story of Mistletoe, Maine, was far from over.

THANK YOU!

Thank you, reader. With so many options, I appreciate your choosing my book to read. Your opinion matters, so please consider sharing a review to help other readers.

BOOK NEWS

Would you like to know when the next book comes out? Click below to sign up for the J.L. Jarvis Journal and get book news, free books, and exclusive content delivered monthly.

news.jljarvis.com

ACKNOWLEDGMENTS

Editing by Red Adept Editing
redadeptediting.com

ABOUT THE AUTHOR

J.L. Jarvis is a left-handed former opera singer/teacher/lawyer who writes books. She now lives and writes on a mountaintop in upstate New York.

jljarvis.com

facebook.com/jljarvis1writer

x.com/JLJarvis_writer

instagram.com/jljarvis.writer

bookbub.com/authors/j-l-jarvis

pinterest.com/jljarviswriter

goodreads.com/5106618.J_L_Jarvis

amazon.com/author/B005GoM2Zo

youtube.com/UC7kodjlaG-VcSZWhuYUUl_Q